TO ENCHANT A HIGHLAND EARL

Heart of a Scot
Book Five

By
COLLETTE CAMERON®

Blue Rose Romance®

Sweet - to - Spicy Timeless Romance®

USA Today Bestselling Author
COLLETTE CAMERON
Sweet-to-Spicy Timeless Romance®

For permission requests, write to the publisher at the address below.
Attn: Permissions Coordinator
info@collettecameronbooks.com
collettecameronbooks.com
eBook ISBN: 978-1-954307-76-6
Print Book ISBN: 978-1-966087-39-7

FREE BOOK!

JOIN MY EXCLUSIVE MAILING LIST
Collette Cameron Newsletter

AND GET A FREE EBOOK!

https://collettecameronbooks.com/freegift

Plus Sneak Peeks, Giveaways, Contests, Exclusive Content, and More... P.S. I promise only good stuff ~ **no** spam!

DEDICATION

For every heroine reading this story and
dreaming of her own kilt-clad Highlander.

ONE

**Scottish Highlands
Mid-January 1721**

Clenching the wadded letter tightly in his fist, Broden pivoted on his heels and tramped the reverse path across the smooth flagstone floor. His boot heels rapped dully off the book-laden shelves and the dark paneled walls of the masculine chamber acting as his library, private sitting room, and study.

His heartbeat whooshed in his ears, a peculiarly muffled tempo, like someone striking a drum covered by a thick pile of blankets.

The fire in the hearth sizzled as occasional droplets of rain survived the treacherous descent down the chimney only to splutter to a quick death. Outside, a deluge poured from the contemptuous pewter-gray clouds as the biting winter wind assailed everything in its path with unrelenting resolve to pummel and saturate.

He supposed he ought to be grateful it wasn't snowing.

A particularly powerful gust buffeted the sturdy rectangular stone house, causing the windowpanes to rattle and the unremarkable man sitting at Broden's desk to cast a wary glance out the rain-splattered glass.

No doubt, Mr. Philibius Oswald, Solicitor, worried about his return journey to Eddleshaugh.

As well he should.

If the weather remained this dismal—a savvy chap would wager on it—Oswald would be obliged to take a room at one of Eddleshaugh's inns. After he and the sorry nag he'd arrived upon had slogged the almost two miles to the township. At this juncture, the much-traveled tracks to Edinburgh and then London would be impassable if the torrent kept up. Given the ashen sky, that seemed certain.

After all, this was January in the Highlands. One could expect rain and snow. Snow and rain. Then more of the same.

Every bit as certain as the intractable weather's continuation was another simple fact: Broden wouldn't extend his hospitality and offer the attorney a bed for the night. Or two or three if the tempest lingered. Not after learning why Oswald had stupidly—*Sassenach idiot*—braved the storm and called unannounced.

An entirely different sort of storm brewed within the cozy study, though no less fierce or ruthless in its fury. As Broden struggled to accept the life-altering news he'd just received— *Goddammit to hell*—anger and disbelief vied for supremacy in every pore. Pores humming and pulsating and expanding in a silent but raucous chorus of strain and vexation.

And the news... A groan of despair almost escaped past his meshed lips. News he'd never conceived nor expected to hear; not in a hundred—no, a thousand—lifetimes.

God's hairy ballocks, he swore irreverently to himself.

Surely, it was a gargantuan mistake. An enormous, colossal error. A careless clerical blunder or a misprint on some long-ago faded, forgotten, and moldy kirk registry. Someone, somewhere *had* to have made a mistake.

He could not be—most assuredly did not *want* to be—the next Earl of Montforth. Plowing his free hand through his hair, he dislodged the ribbon that kept it tied in a queue at his nape. Earl or not, he wasn't donning a ridiculous curling wig or powdering his hair for anyone.

He was not a mincing fop.

"There's nae one else to inherit?" he demanded of the solicitor, aware but beyond caring that the man simply performed his duties.

Dinna kill the messenger and all that twaddin' shite.

The silent reminder to himself did nothing to lessen his ire. His helplessness. The acerbic frustration. The unequivocal feeling of being trapped. Ensnared. *Imprisoned.*

He jabbed a finger toward the man of law, idly noting the dirt packed beneath the man's nails. Earls didn't have dirty fingernails. Or hands. Neither did they muck out stalls, move rocks from grazing, and farm the land. Or chop their own firewood.

"Ye're absolutely—without a *single* doubt—positive ye havena made a mistake?" he asked.

Oswald vacillated for a long blink, his Adam's apple rapidly cresting and sinking like a miniature boat caught upon the tidal surges of a massive, violent storm. And his tiny ship was about to flounder.

"There *is* another distant *English* cousin," the fusty attorney reluctantly confessed. His eyebrows—wiry copperish things with minds of their own and an unfortunate proclivity to wriggle about on his forehead—huddled together over the pronounced bridge of his beaked nose.

"Aye? *And*?" Broden encouraged, grasping at even the

weakest straw. Anything to keep him from plummeting into the loony world of the aristocracy.

"In truth, he's already contacted me in anticipation—" Oswald faltered, realizing he'd disclosed confidential information. His nervous gaze bounced about the room, landing everywhere but on Broden.

So, the other chap thought to inherit.

Interesting.

Convenient?

Could such a blessed thing be arranged?

Suddenly finding the well-thumbed documents before him of acute interest, Mr. Philibius Oswald cleared his throat. "But you, my lord, are indisputably the *next* in line. I informed him as much, unequivocally. You needn't fear he'll supersede you."

"How did he take it?"

"I beg your pardon?" From the solicitor's gaping jaw and buggy eyes, Broden might have asked him when he'd last swived.

"Was he upset?" He was in no temper to dance around the point or use flowery phrases.

"Naturally, he was—ah—somewhat nonplussed." Oswald chose his words with obvious care. "But I believe he understands the rules governing ennoblement, the letters patent, and the specifics of the remainder are beyond our control. Which is to say, he cannot inherit as long as you are alive."

Och, well, there went that idea all to piss.

Broden didn't miss the pinched expression tightening Oswald's thin face as he admitted that fact. The Englishman assuredly would've preferred his countryman inherit the title, rather than an uncouth, lowborn Scot of questionable comportment and an even more questionable liking for the English.

"His name?" he asked, tempering his impatience.

But only just.

"Mr. Edwin Archibald Wiggins McGregor."

Pompous. Traditional. Unimaginative. A worthy Sassenach name, except for the family surname, that was. McGregor, after all, was a derivative of the Gaelic MacGriogair. Scots through and through, no matter how much Oswald would prefer it otherwise.

"*He* attended Oxford," Oswald added with the merest haughty sniff.

La de dah.

"He's well-traveled and already acquainted with several members of the peerage," the attorney droned on as if listing Edwin's stellar attributes ought to impress Broden.

Or did Oswald prattle on to jab a particular point home?

To demonstrate how much more Edwin was qualified for the title?

As Broden didn't give a hog's teat about Edwin Archibald Wiggins McGregor, not even to pity the man his unfortunate third name, Oswald's intentions missed their mark.

"Ye dinna say?" Each word dripping with sarcasm, he schooled his features into a false expression of suitable admiration. "He sounds like a paragon of society."

Och, I've been to England and France, and I count a half dozen Scots lairds as my friends. I dinna suppose the skinny turd cares about that, though.

"Mr. Archibald McGregor is an investor." If Oswald lifted his nose any higher in self-importance, he might well drown when he left the house.

If that meant Broden might be free of the mammoth burden just dumped upon him, he could be persuaded to look the other way and permit the man to suffer the consequence of his arrogance.

That thought brought him reluctantly 'round to the matter at hand once more.

He was an earl. And, by Odin's toes, he very much didn't want to be.

Mouth cinched into a grim, unyielding line, he leveled the solicitor a steely stare.

"Pray tell me, Mr. Oswald, why I am just now learnin' of my change in circumstances via this?" Broden jerked his hand up, uncurling his fingers around the mashed missive with its dangling black ribbon and seal-imprinted crimson wax. "My predecessor died over a year ago."

Oswald, a gangly fellow, all lanky arms and legs and spindly fingers flicked a disinterested look at the balled paper before bringing his keen, hazel gaze up to scrutinize Broden's features. He examined him for an extended moment, taking in his soiled and mended work clothing, scuffed boots, unkempt and unbound hair, and beard-stubbled face as if searching for something.

For what?

"You do bear a vague resemblance to the late earl." He wiggled his twiggy fingers near his angular face. "In the angles and bone structure of your chin and jaw, though your physique is much more...ah..." He lowered his assessing gaze to take in Broden's shoulders and chest. "*Robust.*"

Meaning, his dead kin had most likely been a milksop and a prancing, affected popinjay.

Had he worn stays?

Broden had heard some Englishmen padded their clothing to enhance certain anatomical features and also wore stays to diminish others.

Broden used the occasion to take the solicitor's measure too.

At odds with his fastidious behavior, gravy stains marred

Oswald's buff-toned, wrinkled waistcoat and a shock of fuzzy red-brown hair poked straight up from atop his otherwise bald pate. Almost as if someone had forgotten to shave the rest of the unfortunate man's pointed head.

It rather gave the man the appearance of a paintbrush.

He peered over the round wire-rims of his spectacles. Seemingly unaffected by either Broden's superior size or his obvious vexation, he calmly lifted the corner of another document he'd pulled from his brown leather portfolio.

"Mr. McGregor—?" The lawyer flushed blotchy red. "I beg your pardon."

He noisily cleared his throat and began again.

"*My lord*, the prior earl was most emphatic that in the event of his death, his heir only be notified when it became abundantly clear that the title would not pass to a progeny of his loins. As his wife was with child at the time of his lordship's unfortunate death, prudence demanded postponing the pronouncement of the fifth Earl of Montforth until the babe's birth seven months later."

A bloody Sassenach earl.

How in all of Christendom had such a wholly preposterous thing occurred?

The earldom did lay just inside the British side of the borderlands, but still...

His focus beyond the soggy landscape visible through the windows, Broden scrunched his eyes and rubbed his chin. Wasn't there something he'd heard once about a long-ago relative scampering off with a noble decades before?

Was that the connection?

His mother might recall.

He'd have to ask her after Oswald took his leave.

As the attorney had explained, somewhere in the gnarly,

extended, and complex family tree, Broden and the previous earl had shared ancestral blood.

Where, precisely, was unclear to him.

"I take it the bairn was a wee lass?" Working his thumb across the stiff wax seal, Broden regarded the attorney. There was something about the man that raised his hackles. Something besides him being an Englishman and a slimy solicitor to boot.

In short, he didn't trust the man.

Perhaps a visit to Oswald's London offices was in order.

Oswald sighed as he removed his spectacles and wiped the lenses with a less than pristine handkerchief he'd lifted from his inside coat pocket. "Seven children in nine years and the only surviving offspring are all daughters. Five, to be precise."

Standish had been a busy man, and mayhap not a complete peacock if he sired that many bairns. Or perhaps, he'd just been desperate to beget an heir. A sliver of pity for Standish's wife poked Broden.

"And quite naturally, it did take several months to locate the next male in line for the title," Oswald blathered on. "We exhausted all of our leads in England before resorting to directing our attention to Scotland."

As he tapped a bony finger atop the scarred and scuffed desk, the man's contempt was fairly palpable. He seemed no keener to tell Broden of his new title than he was to learn of the bloody nuisance.

He heartily wished he *hadn't* been found.

"The law is *very* clear, my lord. You...," he glanced down at the page before him, his brow knitted. "Broden Lachlan Errol McGregor, *are* the fifth Earl of Montforth."

Oswald's nasally, clipped tones set Broden's teeth on edge. Not good, considering a very fine tether held his ire in check.

The fire popped and snapped as a log fell, disintegrating

into glowing, crimson-orange coals. More for a need to do something than to build the flames once more, Broden laid the letter atop the mantel beside a bronze candlestick, then knelt and added another log to the blaze. With the poker, he shoved a few coals beneath the new addition, coaxing the fire, and soon hungry flames licked up the sides.

He set the poker in place before planting his palms on his thighs and pushing upright once more, accompanied by a hefty, resigned sigh.

Christ and all the angels would descend from heaven before he trotted himself off to England to claim a Sassenach earldom. *God's teeth.* He could already hear Liam MacKay's and Graeme Kennedy's mocking chortles. Logan Rutherford and Coburn Wallace would be utterly unbearable.

"What if I refuse?"

"*Refuse?* Why... Why... You cannot." Rapidly blinking his eyes owl-like behind his lenses, Oswald spluttered like a stubby candle's flame about to die. "The title *is* yours. *Yours.*"

Yes, definite scorn riddled his terse speech.

"What *you* do with the honor is, of course, up to you. But there is no question of not accepting," the solicitor insisted. "You are the Earl of Montforth until you depart this earth, my lord."

Just because the paperwork *said* he was an earl didn't mean Broden must adjust his life one iota. He leaned a shoulder against the stone mantel—stones which had been cleared from his lands by his two-times-two grandfather—and crossed his arms. "And if I choose to ignore it and continue as I have for the past three decades?"

Oswald raised his bland gaze for a moment before attending to his spectacles once more. Something deep within the depths of his eyes shifted. The briefest flash before he sank his attention to cleaning his eyewear.

"As you can imagine, my lord, Lady Montforth is quite beside herself, awaiting news of her future and that of her children. She is a gentle creature, devoted to her daughters, and the epitome of refinement."

Aye, Broden grudgingly admitted to himself. The countess was in a precarious predicament through no fault of her own.

"The household staff, the tenants, not to mention the villagers, all await your directives." Oswald spoke clearly and deliberately as if striving to make a bacon brain or mutton head understand a complex mathematical formula. "These past months have been a hardship for them all as the stewards and solicitors could only make superficial decisions."

The twig of a man all but implied Broden owed it to those people he'd never met—strangers—to ensure their futures and well-being. He wasn't a selfish man, by God, but to uproot himself and charge off to England? To become part of that uppity set—the haughty aristocrats who looked down their snooty noises upon the Scots?

Nae.

Not as long as he drew a breath.

The familial home he shared with his mother, a cook, a maid of all work, and, on occasion, his childhood friend, Quinn Catherwood, until he'd married last Christmastide, was simple but comfortable.

And the eighteen acres he owned, which fed sheep, a few cows, and other livestock quite nicely. Conveniently, a brook rambled through the northernmost edge of his property, where he enjoyed fishing as time permitted.

He also employed two laborers who tended everything from the garden to the stables, and he worked alongside them at whatever task most needed completing. Hence his dirty nails and soiled garments today.

Broden highly doubted the previous Earls of Montforth

had ever even broken a sweat, let alone cleaned hog sties, dug peat, helped deliver lambs, or used a blade upon another man.

Though he'd never attended a fancy university, Broden was well-educated and knew how to wield a sword and a dirk, thanks to his scholarly father's tutelage. And thanks to his mother, he could maneuver a ballroom when required to dance and spoke a dab of French. When pressed, he could conduct himself like the poshest of gentlemen.

But don the shroud of a noble?

An earl?

Wouldn't that make him the worst sort of hypocrite?

"At the very least, I would expect, your lordship, that you'd *want* to examine your holdings." Oswald rubbed his reedy nose, leaving a faint ink trail down the side. "After all, Sommerley Parke House is not even two days' journey from here."

A better man might've told the man of law about the ink smear.

Broden wasn't such a man.

With the smudge on his thin nose, Oswald resembled an over-sized rodent. Appropriate, since Broden regarded all attorneys as vermin. He had yet to meet one who didn't serve his selfish interests first. Oh, no doubt there were a good number of ethical and honest lawyers in their field. He'd just not had the privilege of meeting one as yet.

"I suppose you could hire a man of business to oversee your estate or expand the duties of your current stewards," Oswald continued, as if thinking aloud, his eyes slightly narrowed and fingers loosely steepled. "The countess did ask me to inquire what your wishes are for her and her daughters —now your wards. Should they remain at Sommerley Parke House? Retire to the dower house? One of the other estates? Bellewaite House? Come here?"

Dower house? Other estates?

Wait, the bloody hell!

Here? Them come here?

Where in God's name would he put six females and no doubt a lady's maid for the countess, a nanny for the youngest girls, a governess for the older lasses, and a nurse for the infant?

"Shite," Broden swore beneath his breath, furious and foul.

The care of the former earl's wife and five daughters were now his responsibility. *Hell and damnation.* He'd never even met Standish, the fourth earl, and certainly never anticipated inheriting.

Inheriting?

Derision curled his lip.

He hadn't even been aware of the title until Oswald, very much appearing like a drowning mongrel, had banged most insistently upon his door two hours ago.

Broden's mother coughed delicately before entering with a laden tray. Her lace cap flapped upon her graying hair as she limped to the low table before a well-worn, sage-green sofa.

Damp weather always made her joints stiffen and ache. Rather than waiting upon him and Oswald, she ought to be snuggled in her bed sipping a hot willow bark and turmeric toddy, heated flannel encasing her legs, and a ripping good book between her work-worn hands.

"Mr. Oswald," she said with a cheery smile, "I'm certain ye must be famished."

Her simple plaid gown and white apron pinned to the front bespoke a woman of gentle but humble means. The McGregors weren't impoverished by any stretch, but neither were they affluent.

Oswald perked up as the aromas of Scotch pies and warm bread wafted from the tray's direction.

"Indeed, Mrs. McGregor. A most welcome respite." Oswald stacked his papers into a neat pile. Once he'd closed the inkpot, he hurried to the sofa and availed himself of a Scotch pie.

Mother poured him a cup of coffee. "Broden, would ye care for coffee?"

"Nae." He strode to his desk and pulled open the bottom drawer. Removing a glass and a whisky bottle, he poured three finger's worth of the dark, amber liquid. Reluctantly, he angled the bottle toward Oswald. "Whisky, Oswald?"

The solicitor lifted his long nose, his nostrils flaring in distaste. "Thank you, no. I've found Scottish spirits are too strong for my palate."

Och, the toff probably takes milk in his coffee too.

Before Broden had finished the thought, Oswald said, "May I impose upon you to add milk to my coffee and three sugar lumps, Mrs. McGregor?"

"Aye." His mother swiftly complied, her right eyebrow elevated. That always meant she had a great deal more to say but had elected to hold her sharp tongue, which could strip a heather bush bare when she was incensed.

Broden, on the other hand, had to bite his tongue to keep from telling the rickle-a-bones his mother wasn't a servant.

A fine line pulling her eyebrows together, his mother peered at him with knowing, pale brown eyes. Eyes very much like his own. The hue not quite the shade of strong tea but more fawn colored. "Are ye no' eatin', Son?"

"I shall later." He dropped a kiss onto the crown of her head as he wrapped an arm around her shoulder. "Why dinna ye rest now? I ken this damp weather wreaks havoc on yer joints."

Her gaze avid with curiosity, she sent the solicitor a considering look.

A wry, mocking smile skewed Broden's mouth at her not-so-subtle hint. "I'll tell ye everythin'—"

"The earldom owns houses in Brighton and London as well," Oswald said between bites and uncouth, appreciative noises. "One of those climes might be beneficial to your health, Mrs. McGregor."

In England?

Not bloody likely.

Broden lanced the man through with his gaze. Did he truly think to manipulate him by playing upon his sympathies?

"Earldom?" His mother's attention swept between the men. "Have ye inherited Standish's title, Broden?"

She knew about the title?

TWO

Laughing out loud, Kendra bent low over Pandora's creamy neck and raced across the moors, her unbound hair streaming behind her. The rain had finally stopped, and the land had dried enough that she dared take a ride today.

Astride!

Mother had permitted the outing if Kendra also rode into Eddleshaugh and picked up the skeins of wool she'd ordered. Never in her memory was there a time Mother wasn't knitting away at something or other.

Since Kendra also needed a length of violet ribbon for the bonnet she was retrimming, and any excuse to be out of doors would suffice, she'd eagerly agreed.

Naturally, Mother had no idea Kendra hadn't dutifully ordered the sidesaddle placed upon Pandora, and the extra coin she slipped the stable lad assured he'd keep her secret.

Both rider and horse panting, she reined the mare to a halt atop a grassy knoll. An appreciative half-smile curving her mouth, she took in the quaint village nestled in the shallow valley below. As much as she enjoyed venturing to Edinburgh and the busy social scene the city afforded, she never tired of this friendly hamlet of her girlhood.

"Let's go, lass."

Clucking her tongue, she nudged the mare's sides with her heels and continued onto the well-worn path from Eytone Hall. Left over from the tempest that had blown through two days ago, the weather remained frigid and blustery. The wind insistently tangled her long hair and whipped bright color onto her cold cheeks.

Out of habit, she scanned the trees on either side of the rutted track. Sane people were tucked up comfortably in their houses. Most animals too.

Singing a naughty ditty loud enough to send a red grouse skyward from the cover of a clump of heather, she cast a cautious glance overhead. A few charcoal-colored clouds hovered on the horizon. Though it was bitterly cold, the outdoors was a welcome reprieve to Eytone Hall's confines.

As Pandora clopped along, entering the woodlands that preceded the small township, Kendra scrunched her eyebrows and her singing trailed off.

There was that unnerving sensation again.

That undefinable restlessness.

An edginess she couldn't put an exact name to, but which came increasingly more often in recent days. Unfamiliar discontentment had niggled for weeks now. And confound it all, she couldn't quite put her finger on the reason.

She wasn't lonely or bored.

Yet a disquiet had entered her spirit, discomfited her soul, and disrupted her peace of mind. And of late, she'd found herself staring off into space or woolgathering about nonsensical silliness. Silliness that heretofore hadn't beleaguered her.

Mainly, what would it be like to have a husband? Children? To be mistress of her own home? To have a man gaze at her with hot passion simmering in his eyes? To feel his mouth and large hands upon her body? Her bare skin? His sinewy weight atop her?

For certain, in part, her fantasies might be attributed to her brother Liam Mackay, Baron of Penderhaven's recent marriage. And their cousin Skye had married Quinn Catherwood Christmas day too.

As it frequently had since their weddings, her mind turned to her unwed state.

At twenty, some might consider her past her prime.

She, however, wasn't one of them.

Honestly, she'd hadn't given her marriage a whole lot of thought until lately. Oh, on occasion, Mother would murmur something about Kendra settling down, but she still wasn't in any hurry to exchange vows.

Chiefly, since she'd yet to meet a man who interested her *that* way. Neither Mother nor Liam seemed inclined to force her into exchanging vows either. Most probably, Liam's awful first marriage had a great deal to do with that blessing.

Broden McGregor's ruggedly striking features pushed to the forefront of her mind. One of her brother's closest friends, she'd known him since she was a wee lass. He'd been a sharp sliver buried in her heel and paining her for that long as well.

Five or six years ago, while he and Liam had shared a bottle of whisky in the library, she'd overheard him refer to her as a splotchy-faced dumpling with perpetually knotted hair and grubby smudges on her chubby cheeks. He'd laughed before adding, "I've never kent a lass who eats more sweets. I feel sorry for her pony."

For a girl hopelessly infatuated with the too-bloody-handsome-for-his-own-good man, his words had wounded her to the core. Each had lanced deeply. And each had inflicted a gaping sore, ripped her youthful self-confidence to shreds, and left her uncertain—then and now—that any man would ever desire her.

She'd secretly cried herself to sleep for a fortnight and had promptly given up all manner of sweets and the like. She rarely indulged in them now, afraid those excessive, round curves of her youth would reappear—to once more make her an object of scorn and ridicule.

Truthfully, and to be fair, she had been plump as a partridge, with a penchant for getting into scrapes, and cared not a whit about her appearance. Her complexion had been horrid and spotty for two entire years too.

Kendra might've only been a child at the time, and Broden had been well into his cups. Nonetheless, his words had an enduring effect on her.

After hearing his slurred, unkind pronouncements, she'd stopped finagling excuses to come upon him and Liam. In fact, she'd begun avoiding Broden as much as possible, a habit she often employed now as well.

From her observations, she was the only woman to do so. Lasses flung themselves at him, and he took their worship and adoration in his masculine stride. As if it were his due.

Arrogant devil.

Snorting, she shook her head, causing her hair to swirl around her shoulders.

"*Broden McGregor.* A royal pain in my backside. When I do take a husband, he'll be nothin' like that great conceited lout. He'll think I'm the most splendid thing he's ever set eyes upon because he'll love me."

Flaws and all.

Pandora raised and dipped her head, almost in a nod of agreement.

Kendra made a rude noise in the back of her throat. Now Broden only succeeded in pricking her temper every time they were in the same room together, and she struggled to recall precisely what she'd found so attractive about him in her youth.

Why Liam counted him such a great friend, she would never appreciate. Perhaps because he'd never had a brother and both of Broden's had died. Liam and Broden had been dear friends since boyhood. Mother said boys needed other boys about to tussle with. They formed bonds women couldn't understand, the same way women formed bonds with each other.

The mare whickered softly and shook her head, shying away from the swaying branches of a nearby bush.

"Shh." Kendra soothed Pandora with a calming hand to her warm neck.

It wasn't like the mare to be skittish.

She scrutinized the familiar area, noting nothing unusual. Unlike other parts of the Highlands, which still dealt with tribal strife, bandits, and occasional issues with the gypsies traveling through, this area remained untroubled by those inconveniences.

Good thing, too, else her mother and Liam would never permit her to ride to Eddleshaugh alone. To her knowledge, no one had ever been robbed or assaulted within thirty miles of Eytone Hall.

Nonetheless, disquiet prickled between her shoulder blades, and a shudder scuttled down her spine. Shivering against the increasingly icy wind, she pulled the mantle's hood over her head, grateful for the fine, protective fabric.

The wool to make the cloth had come from Liam's sheep. Not that Kendra or her mother spun the wool. Neither possessed the talent or, at least in Kendra's case, had no desire to learn the craft.

She doubted her mother did either. No, the Dowager

Baroness of Penderhaven's interest in wool consisted of what she'd knit next.

A rider approached from the direction of the village. Raising a hand to cover her eyes against an inconvenient ray of sun determined to blind her, she squinted into the distance.

Blast and bother.

Bunions and boils.

Ballocks and...and...and blisters.

A muffled noise escaped her lips as she forcibly exhaled a frustrated breath.

Of all the rotten luck and wholly undesirable people to encounter.

She well knew the burly form so casually exuding masculine grace atop Sheik, Broden's light chestnut gelding with its distinct blond mane and tail.

How many times had she seen Broden's wide shoulders that easily filled a door frame? Or those ridiculously muscled thighs sprawled out before a fire? Or flexing as he danced or wrestled with her brother or one of their friends?

Not, she reminded herself sternly, that his physical attributes meant anything to her. She simply made objective observations.

What a colossal lie. Bald-faced and self-deceiving. Self-protecting too, in point of fact.

With an unyielding resolve to ignore the unwelcome sensations having the audacity to flit about behind her ribs at the sight of him, she swallowed. What she felt was annoyance. Absolutely—*absolutely*—nothing more.

Liar, that damned, vexing little voice whispered again with a distinct note of glee.

Fine then: irritation, aggravation, and exasperation as well.

Could one's conscience snort in disbelief?

Kendra *did* admire Broden's masculine form. What

woman with eyes in her head and a pulse beating in her veins would not?

She itched to skim her fingers over those granite shoulders and marble thighs—had ever since coming upon him, Liam, and Quinn swimming stark naked in the loch. Heat suffused her cheeks at the vivid memory.

Praise be to the saints that Liam and Quinn had already dove into the water. Only Broden had stood atop the projecting rock, his glorious back, buttocks, and thighs dripping with water and deliciously bare to her curious and avid scrutiny.

Even as a child, she'd recognized he was as beautiful as a carved statue: all sculpted hard curves and magnificent planes and angles.

She'd never quite been able to erase that image from her mind, even when she was most peeved with him. Which was aggravatingly frequent. And, to her utter consternation, many, many, *many* times over the past years, his glorious, unsettling, and superb form had interrupted her dreams.

They'd been the focus of a myriad of daydreams too.

Self-disgust and self-castigation at her fickleness stomped dual feet upon her pride.

Broden drew to a halt beside her, his celestial smile flashing across his sun-kissed face.

She'd always liked his smile; the way the devilish slant lit his umber-brown eyes and warmed the atmosphere. And despite her determination otherwise, that sinful mouth still had the power to send wickedly delightful chills scampering down her spine.

Stupid, stupid girl. It was just teeth and lips.

Aye, but what glorious teeth and lips. What would it be like—?

Kendra firmly quashed the thought before it had a chance

to fully manifest. To her consternation, it was neither a novel nor infrequent thought, *damn my eyes*.

"Good mornin', lass." Must his merry eyes twinkle with whatever that was? As if he could read her thoughts and recognized the feelings he stirred in her? "What brings ye out on this fine day?"

"I'm pickin' up yarn for Mother." And she didn't wish to be delayed by a suave, distracting devil.

He wore buckskins today rather than trews, the legs tucked into boots reaching mid-calf. His black cloak trailed over his expansive shoulders and fell in long waves over his mount's sides. Instead of wearing a tam, a cocked hat topped his sandy-brown hair, worn long and tied at his nape with a black ribbon.

Black gloves encased his fingers, which she knew to be thick and strong. He raised his hand to scratch just left of his mouth. Stubble shadowed his jaw as if he hadn't shaved in a day or two.

Instead of making him appear unkempt or slovenly, the beard gave him a roguish, pirate-like appearance. As if he needed anything to make him more attractive. Not that she was foolish enough to fall into *that* trap ever again.

Why, *blast it*, was she even noticing?

Hadn't she spent years diligently recounting his many faults?

Broden McGregor was a womanizing flirt.

Once before, he'd burned Kendra. *Badly.* She still bore the scars, deep in her soul. She'd not make that mistake twice. Shifting slightly in her saddle, she stifled the unwanted fluttering in her belly as his approving gaze took in her exposed knees and calves.

If he told Liam...

A groan almost escaped her.

No. She wouldn't show weakness. Not to him. She jutted her chin upward and squared her shoulders in a silent challenge.

"I take it yer brother and mother arena aware ye intended to ride astride?" he murmured, humor ringing in his deep voice.

Curse him for reading her mind again.

"Nae, and I'd appreciate it if ye didna mention it." She hated asking him for a favor, but she so coveted her rides. "They'd restrict my outin's to sedate trails, properly sittin' atop a sidesaddle, and with a groom for a chaperone."

Oddly, warmth and amusement glinted in his whisky-colored eyes, rather than the irritation, impatience, and exasperation that typically showed there when he gazed upon her.

They'd had more than one silent battle, glaring daggers at each other. And many more verbal spats, sparring with snipes and innuendos, and occasionally outright rudeness.

But today, he seemed in an uncommonly benevolent mood, which made her suspicious.

"What brings ye to town so early?" she asked, hoping to steer his hot, acute gaze from her legs. The clock hadn't chimed a quarter past eight when she'd galloped Pandora from Eytone Hall's stables.

The mare shook her head and backstepped, but Kendra brought her back under control.

Something inscrutable flitted across his face before he shifted his attention to a point somewhere beyond her shoulder. "I had correspondences that required postin'."

A servant might've completed the task, but so might a footman have collected Mother's wool skeins. Likely, Broden was as eager to seek the outdoors and take advantage of the break in the weather as she'd been.

In that way, they were alike. Both craved the outdoors and

loathed being confined and cooped up inside. In the Highlands, one took the opportunity to partake of fresh air when it presented itself during the winter months. Such comfortable days were few and far between.

"Well, I'd best be on my way. I wouldna want my mother to fret if I'm away longer than she expects. Good day to ye, Mr. McGregor." With a polite dip of her chin, she urged Pandora around him.

"*Mr. McGregor*?" He chuckled at the formality, and, at once, ire stiffened her back.

The infuriating man was forever laughing at her. Since she was a young girl trailing after him, Liam, and Quinn, he'd teased her, mocked her, and gone out of his way to be a royal pain in the arse.

Not cruel or vicious. Except for that single time that Kendra had overheard him.

What if...? What if that hadn't been the only time he'd disparaged her? Could he have voiced his negative opinions regularly? And if so, why hadn't Liam done anything about it?

The thought made her hot and cold at once and utterly mortified. And angry. Blood-scorching angry.

No longer was she an insecure, self-conscious child worshiping the very ground he trod upon. The blustery wind carried her patience away as easily as thistledown, and she swung around to give him a proper set down.

Her breath stalled and cramped in her lungs as shock rendered her speechless. Jaw slack, she stared horrified into the trees, momentarily unable to move or speak.

Nae. Nae. Nae!

There amongst the fluctuating shadows, partially concealed by the trees' roughened trunks, sat a man astride a horse. His lower face covered with a grungy handkerchief, he aimed a pistol straight at Broden.

Dear God!

That was why Pandora had been edgy. She'd sensed his presence. Probably had smelled the other horse. And like an idiot, Kendra had disregarded her intuition and the horse's warnings.

Shaking loose the icy paralysis crippling her, Kendra jabbed a finger toward the gunman, screaming, "Broden, he has a—"

The explosion boomed through the chilly air.

Birds took to wing in a frantic flurry.

Rearing onto her hind legs, Pandora neighed in terror.

The echo of pounding hoofbeats filtered through the ringing in Kendra's ears as she battled to stay atop the frightened horse.

The poltroon had made good his escape.

Blackguard. Fiend. Bloody coward.

Heart pounding louder than a battering ram against a keep's door, Kendra fought to bring the mare under control. After several tense seconds, she succeeded and reined Pandora swiftly toward Broden.

Cold sweat pooled under her arms, terror yet clawing at her mind and throat.

He sat slightly hunched over but still in the saddle, thank God.

She'd never have been able to lift him back atop his horse. She swallowed the acerbic bile burning her throat and attempted to ignore the flurry of a thousand wings beating hysterically at her belly and behind her ribs.

Oh, God.

She swallowed reflexively.

When she'd seen that evil man, the gun's barrel pointed straight at Broden. When the shock and terror had rendered her immobile.

"Broden," she breathed, scraping her frantic gaze over him, noting his strained, white-as-chalk-face. "Are ye...?" She wet her lower lip, willing the waves of nausea to subside. Forcing her tongue to form the hated words. "Are ye *shot*?"

Rigid lines scored the hard planes of his face. He pressed one palm to his chest, just to the right of his left collarbone. A dark substance oozed between the black leather of his gloves.

Blood.

Jesus, help me.

Broden's blood.

Dizzying faintness assailed Kendra, and she blinked rapidly, fighting to stay conscious. Clenching the pommel, she gulped in long, ragged breaths. She couldn't abide the sight of blood. For as long as she could recall, it had always made her lightheaded and queasy.

She could not faint.

She could not.

I shall no'.

He needed her to be strong, not a swooning numpty.

With gritty resolve, she rallied her composure and dug in her pocket for a handkerchief. She thrust it at Broden. "Here. Ye need to staunch the flow. Press hard."

She didn't know where she'd acquired that knowledge, but now wasn't the time to ponder the source. Neither could she look at the widening circle for fear she'd dissolve into vapors before she saw him to safety.

For she must do so.

There was no one else close enough to lend him a hand, and he bled badly.

His mouth quirked the merest bit at the delicate lace-edged accessory before accepting it. Along with his own, he folded the cloth into a neat square and pressed them inside his cloak.

"Broden, we must see ye back to Eytone Hall. 'Tis closer than yer house."

His face a ghastly shade of white, he grimaced as he pulled an eight-inch ballock dagger from a leather sheath within his boot. "Ye might need this, lass. Do ye ken how to use it?"

"Aye," she choked out, emotion blossoming behind her breastbone.

Here he slumped, blood gushing from his wound, and he worried about her safety?

Perhaps, just perhaps, he wasn't quite the evil ogre she'd imagined him to be.

"Who would want to shoot ye?" She swallowed a gulp, gazing at the steel hilt, glinting faintly in the filtered light. She yanked up her gown and used the blade to help tear a long strip of a petticoat as she puzzled over who could want him dead.

Everyone adored Broden. Revered him even. Men and women alike. *Especially the women.* Townsfolk, clansmen, old crones, and toddlers adored the man.

Even in Edinburgh, amongst the toplofty nobles and snooty aristocrats, his keen intellect and warrior's skills drew the appreciation of the males. As usual, the females fairly drooled over him.

Rich and poor. Servant and lord. Every blasted person worshipped Broden McGregor.

Everyone except Kendra MacKay, that was.

"I dinna ken," he muttered, reminding her she'd asked him a question.

He wavered in the saddle, and, in a blink, she made a decision.

She couldn't risk him toppling from his horse, and there was no way in all of Christendom she would leave him and ride for help. Not with the would-be killer possibly lurking nearby ready to finish him off.

A wave of icy fear swept from her waist, up her sides, and streaked out across her shoulders and arms, raising her flesh.

I heard him ride away, she shakily reassured herself.

Yes, but how far?

For how long?

Even now, might he be reloading his pistol?

Might he come back to finish the job?

She slid from Pandora's back, then looped her reins through Sheik's girth straps and tied them off. The sheath he'd given her wouldn't fit in her pocket, so she slid it inside her boot before offering him the piece of her petticoat.

"Here. This should help stop the bleedin'."

He accepted the cloth and added it to their handkerchiefs, then pressed his scarlet hand firmly to his stained cloak. Leading the gelding to a fallen log, Kendra clambered into the saddle behind him. She must put distance between Broden and his would-be assassin.

If the man should return...

Or if Broden lost too much blood...

Nae. Dinna think on, either.

"What do ye think ye're doin', lass?" His words were slightly slurred, his light-brown eyes framed by lush lashes, unfocused as he peered at her over his hard-as-marble shoulder.

She had to hurry and pray she was strong enough to keep him before her as they rode to Eytone Hall.

"Savin' yer worthless life, ye big oaf."

THREE

The worst and longest minutes of Broden's life passed as he battled to stay conscious. If he succumbed to the tempting blackness beckoning at the periphery of his mind, Kendra wasn't strong enough to keep him before her.

She, of course, would chew hot coals before admitting that truth, stubborn lass.

Even now, he could feel her arms straining to help support him as she steered Sheik, Pandora docilely keeping pace beside them.

A low groan escaped Broden despite his effort to smother the sound, and he gritted his teeth against another vision-blurring, gut-wrenching stab of scorching pain.

He'd feared Kendra would faint dead away when she'd first spotted the bloody front of his cloak. He remembered well her penchant for swooning if she saw anything remotely gory.

Yet, she'd rallied valiantly. Brilliantly, in fact. Like a warrior, she'd set her mind to the task, ignoring her discomfort.

Even in his miserable state, he couldn't help but admire her stoicism.

Her determined chin and set jaw. The way she'd cleverly dealt with her horse before clambering onto Sheik's back. Her remarkable ability to control her fear and see to the task at hand.

Namely, saving him.

At that precise moment, Sheik stepped into a slight rut, thrusting Broden's and Kendra's bodies forward. Her shapely thighs flexed against his hips as she balanced herself and him, sending a jolt of incinerating desire straight to his groin.

A half-hiss, half-oath escaped between his gritted teeth.

"I'm verra sorry, Broden." She cinched her slender arms tighter around his waist, which also caused her luscious breasts to press into his back—the damned firm nipples teasing and taunting sensuously. "I'm tryin' to be careful. I ken ye're in much pain."

She believed his groans and oaths were pain-induced. Some were, but the torture of his body responding to her innocent touch nearly drove him mad with carnal desire.

Desire? Nae.

Nothing so timid.

What bubbled inside him was raging lust. Pure unadulterated, unappeased, unrequited lust. For the impossibly frustrating, undeniably exquisite Kendra MacKay.

Siren. Sorceress. Forbidden fruit.

"Dinna fash yerself," he managed through clamped teeth.

They'd crack along with his entire jaw if he clenched them any harder. But he'd not show weakness before this courageous lass. Neither would she ever know how much he wanted her.

He sent a thankful prayer heavenward she hadn't clambered onto the saddle before him, or the very hard, very aroused, and very noticeable cockstand bulging at his groin would've swiftly apprised her of his true condition.

Not that he didn't feel awful as hell from the bullet hole to his chest.

Or was it his shoulder?

Somewhere in between was his best guess without stripping off his clothing to take a look.

If Kendra hadn't warned him, he wouldn't have had time to shift his stance at all. He very well might've taken the ball in the head. In point of fact, he hadn't even had time to ponder who would've attempted to kill him yet. And, by God what was more, who had been stupid enough to shoot him in front of a witness?

Those questions could be answered later.

When he could cobble together more than one thought. When every bit of his fuzzy focus and every ounce of his waning strength wasn't on staying awake and atop his horse.

Christ on the blessed cross.

Was Kendra in danger now too?

She'd seen the gunman. Broden hadn't.

Dragging in shallow breaths—to inhale deeply simply hurt too badly—he concentrated on staying upright. Well, as upright as possible.

His pride smarted in no small manner.

Never having been shot before, he'd not considered how he'd respond, but he'd like to have believed better than this. It felt as if a hot poker burned non-stop in his chest and shoulder. Pathetically weak, freezing, and his stomach waffy from the loss of blood, he truly feared he'd pass out cold.

He'd prefer a stab wound. Those types of injuries he was familiar with. *Aye.* Didn't his body bear several scars from blades?

He sucked in an unsteady breath through his mouth.

God save him, how he longed to surrender to the blessed darkness. To be rid of the permeating pain.

But Kendra would be frantic if he tumbled from the horse. She wouldn't leave him. He knew it beyond a doubt. And until the blackguard who shot him was apprehended, she was in as much danger as he.

"Ye're doin' splendidly," she soothed into his ear, her warm breath a delicate caress. "Just a little farther, and ye can rest. We'll send for the physician. In nae time, ye'll be plucky as a fat goose."

The whole while, she'd murmured words of encouragement. Not at all what Broden had expected from the prickly lass. She kept Sheik to a brisk, steady pace but hadn't sent him into a gallop or trot.

Likely because she knew full well that she wouldn't be able to keep him in the saddle if she did. She probably fretted the pounding movements might cause more blood loss too.

Which was bloody worse?

The hole in him or the soft, ripe mounds torturing him from behind? How many times had he yearned to touch those full, tempting pillows? The luscious curves that were forever off-limits to him?

Kendra was Liam's cherished younger sister.

And she abhorred Broden.

She mustn't ever know how much he wanted her. Not ever.

He did have his pride, after all.

Thank the divine powers that she'd never know arousal caused half of his tortured moans. With her strong thighs cradling his arse, the tantalizing length of slim legs revealed for his admiration, her bosom bouncing against his back, and her light and delicate camellia and lemony fragrance nearly driving him out of his mind, he was as randy as a stag in full rut.

A stag who'd been shot.

She'd be livid if she knew. Might even shove Broden off his

horse and leave him to die in the heather lining the rutted track.

Kendra MacKay held him in the lowest of regard.

It hadn't always been thus.

He clearly remembered the awkward, little hoyden trailing after him and her brother, hiding in draperies and eavesdropping, popping out from behind bushes, a ready grin on her round face, her hair tousled about her and usually dirt smudges on her cheeks or chin.

Then, one day, she'd just stopped.

No hiding. No giggles. No impish smiles.

She'd never attempted to follow her brother or him again. In fact, afterward, he'd often visit and never set his eyes upon her. Almost as if she avoided him on purpose.

At first, he'd been relieved. As a man of three and twenty, Kendra's obvious, youthful infatuation had made him uncomfortable. She was a child, for God's sake. The beloved younger sister of his closest friend.

He'd done his utmost to kindly discourage her for years and yet was puzzled by her sudden absence. Odd that all at once, she appeared to have comprehended and took to heart the hints he'd liberally dispensed for so long.

Later, he grudgingly admitted to himself that he'd missed her. Her precocious questions and dove-gray eyes wide with wonderment. Her unfettered laughter and mischievous antics. She'd been a delightful, brazen, spirited lass with a swift, playful smile and a keen mind. And an insatiable curiosity and joy for life.

Of course, once she'd bloomed into the sable haired, ivory-skinned, bowed lipped, scrumptiously curved woman now struggling to keep him in the saddle before her, he'd coveted her attention once more. Coveted a great deal more, in truth.

More of her forbidden fruit.

And wasn't it just like a man to desire what he couldn't have? What he'd deliberately put from him all those years ago?

Wee Kendra had grown into an exquisite woman.

A woman he'd observed many a man watching with a less than brotherly intent. How many times had he tamped down the urge to throttle a chap for overstepping? For daring to turn a lewd or lustful eye upon her? For remarking to another insolent whelp what he'd like to do with her lush form?

The same damned things Broden longed to do to her, God curse him.

But she'd never shown any degree of warmth toward him these past several years. The reverse was true. Icy and aloof, she seemed to detest his presence as if he'd somehow offended her.

And how they bickered and quarreled. Constantly, and over the most trivial and mundane things. Stupid, inconsequential things. Each one vying to win the current battle they were engaged in.

Like an ill-suited husband and wife.

Only Kendra Eislyn Olive MacKay could set his teeth on edge, ignite a wildfire in his blood, and burrow beneath his skin, causing him to behave like a recalcitrant schoolboy.

"We're nearly there, Broden." She gave his waist the merest nudge, worry tinging her low voice when he didn't respond. "I see Eytone Hall's chimney stacks. Do ye?"

He opened his eyes a fraction, squinting at the mansion, as familiar to him as his own much humbler house. The difference in their stations had never mattered to him and Liam. Now Broden had come into a bloody earldom and outranked Liam. And according to Oswald, he was damn wealthy too.

Perhaps even suitable to court a baron's sister?

The irony didn't escape him.

Even in his weakened state, the idea brought a reluctant grin to his mouth.

"Broden? Do ye see Eytone?" Near panic had leeched into her voice.

"Aye," he said, through the gravel clogging his throat.

Raising his head took too much effort, so he peered through his half-open eyes. Pray God, someone from the house would spot them, or else he had no idea how they'd dismount.

"Simmons! Liam!" Kendra shouted at the top of her voice as soon as they'd clattered into the courtyard. "We need help."

The manor's double doors flew open.

Prince, Liam's huge mongrel, bounded down the stairs, woofing a greeting. At once, he sensed something was amiss and began whining as he circled the horses and sniffed Broden's feet.

The butler said something over his shoulder into the entry before hurrying down the stairs too. In all the years Broden had visited Eytone Hall, he'd never once witnessed Simmons moving faster than a sedate, perfectly-measured stride.

In his haste to reach them, the servant actually trotted.

Trotted, by God.

"What's happened?" Liam descended the risers two at a time. He reached Sheik, and, forehead furrowed in concern, swept his pewter gaze between Kendra and Broden. He put a hand on Broden's knee. "Ye look bloody awful, my friend."

Only Kendra's presence kept Broden from telling him to sod off.

He might very well vomit on him still, however.

Liam's wife, Emeline, and his mother, Louisa, took one look at Broden. Both went pale as milk as they, too, scurried from the house.

"Good Laird and all the blessed saints," the dowager whispered upon seeing his blood-saturated front. "My poor, dear lad."

Emeline wrapped an arm around her mother-in-law to steady her. "Oh, Broden," she whispered, then bit her lip, her distress as palpable as the dowager's.

"He's been shot, Liam." Kendra's voice shook slightly and, not for the first time, Broden acknowledged what stoicism and bravery she'd shown.

He'd likely have died if it weren't for her courage and quick thinking.

Nonetheless, known for his wicked charm, Broden attempted to lighten the situation and wipe the solemn expressions from everyone's faces.

"The good news is, thanks to yer sister, the gunman missed his mark." Dizziness assailed him as he turned his head to glance at Kendra. "I'm surprised she warned me, considerin' how she feels about me."

Shock registered on her alabaster pale features, and something more glimmered in her wide, dove-gray eyes, the sooty lashes lowering to half-mast to hide the emotion.

Hurt? Disbelief? Accusation?

Her pretty, plump mouth compressed into a thin ribbon as she accepted her brother's assistance from the saddle. "Someone needs to go for the physician at once."

The fact that she didn't blister his ears or offer a sharp retort bespoke much of his weakened condition. Kendra would never kick someone when they were down. But just wait until he'd recovered.

"I'll see to it, Miss." Simmons rushed to a hovering footman who nodded briskly before setting off toward the stables at a full run.

Dowager Penderhaven called to Simmons. "Have Mrs. Pottager prepare a chamber at once. We'll also need hot water and bandages. And whisky."

Aye. An entire bottle will do.

With a brisk nod, the butler disappeared inside the house.

Laying a palm atop Broden's forearm, as if he feared he might keel over at any moment, Liam asked, "Can ye walk?"

Nae.

Not without falling face-first into the drive.

"Aye." Broden's male pride wouldn't let him show weakness in front of Kendra. Well, further weakness, that was. "If ye can give me a hand..."

He swung his leg over the saddle and pretty much crumpled into an undignified heap as he slid from Sheik. Liam caught him, and Broden couldn't prevent the groan from filtering past his meshed lips. "Can ye let my mother ken? Also, I dinna want her to stay home alone until we ken who did this."

He already had a pretty damn good idea.

"Aye." Liam slanted his chin at a stable hand. "Ready a coach and make for the McGregor's straightaway. Fetch Mrs. McGregor." He glanced at Broden, swaying on his feet. "Dinna tell her Broden's been shot. Just say there's been an accident, and she needs to be prepared to stay at Eytone Hall for a few days."

"Aye, sir."

"Take four men with ye to remain and act as guards too." Liam looped his arm behind his back, and a footman did the same on the other side. "Why would anyone want to shoot ye, Broden?"

Attempting to ignore the increasing buzzing in his ears and the thousands of black and gray dots cavorting before his eyes, Broden summoned a cocky grin. "Why, because I'm the newly titled fifth Earl of Montforth."

Liam jerked his head around to gape. "Are ye serious? Ye're an earl?"

"An earl?" repeated Kendra, astonishment mixing with

the anxiousness in her soft, smoky eyes, that cloud of dark hair billowing around her in the persistent wind.

"Aye, an English earl," he muttered through thick lips, as he, at last, gave in to the weight of his eyelids and slid into nothingness.

FOUR

After a deliciously long and relaxing soak in a lemon and camellia oil-scented bath, Kendra now sat before the robust fire in her chamber brushing her hair dry. She'd dismissed her maid, Olna, needing time alone to unwind and ponder the day's incredible events.

She'd faced two of her worst fears—blood and a wound—and emerged, if not unscathed, then at least triumphant. She hadn't crumpled into a swoon or vomited. No, she'd marshaled her gumption and did what needed doing.

As she stroked her hair, one long glide after another through her damp tresses, she closed her eyes. When the image of the man pointing his gun at Broden invaded her meditations, she popped her eyelids open at once.

That awful picture wouldn't soon leave her memory. If ever.

Her mouth went dry as parchment, just as it had in the woodlands, and a shiver of fear rippled up her spine like waves rushing ashore, raising goose flesh high and taut.

So many unanswered questions ran through her mind, one after the other in rapid succession.

What if Broden hadn't stopped to speak to her?

Would he still have been shot?

How had whoever shot him known he'd be on the road at that time?

What if she hadn't been near to help him?

Would he have died?

That last unpleasant thought sat in her stomach, a hard, aching, miserable knot.

Oh, the man infuriated her to no end. But in all of her memory, there'd never been a time he wasn't around. A brief horse or carriage ride away. His wickedly low and frequent chuckles, echoing in his wide chest. His rumbling brogue reverberating inside Eytone Hall. His treacle-brown eyes flashing with one devilment or another.

She brought a hand to her throat, feeling the fluttering of her pulse beneath her fingertips.

Broden dead? Gone? Forever?

Her heart cramped, taking on an irregular rhythm. *Nae.* 'Twas inconceivable.

Why, try as she might, she couldn't envision a world without him in it. If he were absent, nothing could fill the space that had been him. Nothing, and no one. That sphere would remain empty, void, tragically hollow until the end of time.

Her mood distinctly more somber and pensive, she resumed brushing her hair.

Dr. Haines had come and expertly extracted the ball from Broden's shoulder, which he said hadn't penetrated deeply nor damaged bone or muscle.

Conveniently, Broden had remained insensate during the removal. Although he'd lost a great deal of blood, the physician expected him to recover. *If* he stayed abed and heeded orders to rest.

"He's hale and hearty, and as stubborn a Scot as there is," the doctor said in his thick burr while cleansing his medical instruments in the washbasin. "We must watch for infection and fever, of course."

He'd turned a gimlet eye on Broden, pale and vast against the pillows, a bandage wrapped around his chest and shoulder. "I expect he'll no' be a passive patient. I might have to resort to dosin' him with laudanum if he refuses to cooperate and stay in bed."

Indeed. Dr. Haines hit the mark straight on with that assessment. Broden wouldn't take well to lying abed for any length of time.

Kendra wasn't above tying him to the four posts if he refused to cooperate.

Promising to return every day to check on Broden's progress, the doctor had left instructions with Mrs. McGregor, Emeline, and Mother regarding his care. It rather piqued her that they'd excluded her.

Hadn't she shown she could handle a bit of blood?

Maeve McGregor had arrived a couple of hours ago. At this very moment, she sat beside her only living son's bed, holding his hand and waiting for him to awaken. *And praying.* Praying as only a mother could for her son.

Mother had deemed it prudent to assign Mrs. McGregor a chamber near Broden's, and the kindly woman had taken her dinner in his bedchamber as well. She was grateful to be allowed to nurse her son, but her discomfort at being obligated to the MacKays was tangible.

When she'd learned Broden had been shot, she'd buried her wizened face in her hands and wept. She'd already buried two sons. The poor woman had no one else.

After a thorough interrogation by Liam in the rose salon, requiring Kendra to impart every single detail she could possibly recall about the shooter: his horse, how he sat upon his mount, what he'd been wearing, the kind of gun he wielded, how he held the pistol, even the handkerchief covering his face and the color of his eyes, she had been permitted to seek her chamber.

Not, however, before receiving hearty hugs from her brother, mother, and sister-in-law.

"My bonnie, brave girl," Mother murmured throatily. She shook her dark head, her gray eyes, so like Kendra's and Liam's, brimming with unshed tears. "I canna hardly fathom what ye've gone through this day. Och, and how brave ye've been, my girl."

Liam nodded, rubbing his nape with one hand. "In all likelihood, Kendra, ye did indeed save Broden's life. I confess, I'm puzzled why someone would shoot him. Everyone loves and admires the man."

Kendra barely refrained from rolling her eyes. In point of fact, however, she'd had similar thoughts, and what Liam said was true. Broden was utterly charming to everyone. Everyone, that was, except her.

Emiline, a twinkle in her pretty eyes, gave Kendra an almost teasing smile. "And here I believed ye couldna abide the mon."

"What should I have done?" Eyebrows arched, Kendra shrugged. "Let him die?"

"Of course no'," Emeline swiftly reassured, casting Liam an inquisitive glance.

Must they make more of this than it was?

"Besides," Kendra said, "'tis no' that I dislike Broden. 'Tis that he's able to irritate me as nae one else can, and I dinna like bein' vexed continually. And I do believe the mon goes out of his way to do so, merely to goad a reaction from me."

"Aye, darlin', and ye so easily respond to his teasin'," Mother said, not unkindly.

Kendra did, in fact, but she didn't appreciate having the truth pointed out to her.

Mother's expression turned speculative, and she opened her mouth, then snapped it shut. Nonetheless, she regarded Kendra with slightly narrowed eyes, as if she'd stumbled upon a secret she wasn't quite ready to share with the others.

For certain, Kendra would like to know whatever it was. Maybe then she'd understand the man lying unconscious upstairs. Understand why she couldn't expunge him from her mind despite her determination to do so. Even when she knew full well what he thought of her. Even when she was at odds with him most of the time.

Tossing her head to fling her hair behind her, she squared her shoulders. "For all we ken, the shooter was a cuckolded husband bent on revenge."

The thought made her positively ill, and her empty stomach sank with the weight of fresh nausea.

"Nae." Liam choked on a laugh, shaking his head. "I highly doubt that. Ye dinna ken him as I do."

What? He didn't dally with married women? He saved his cavorting for...? *Who?* Strumpets? Widows? Actresses?

Kendra couldn't quite identify why the light teasing miffed her. She made no bones about her feelings toward Broden. If her family meant to imply something else went on between her and the great lout lying abed upstairs, then they were sorely—*sorely*—mistaken.

She'd done what any decent human being would do when another person was hurt.

After an eternity, but which had only in fact been a few more minutes, she finally excused herself. Before she made a sharp retort or unkind remark to her family. Her patience had long since evaporated, and she'd gone past the point of polite ripostes.

Truth to tell, she'd been utterly petrified she wouldn't reach Eytone Hall in time.

Or that the murderer would pursue them.

She had never been so terrified in her life. Still, she hadn't swooned at the sight of so much blood, and she'd been able to deliver Broden safely to the house. Those were no small accomplishments.

Evidently, as concerned as she was that the shooter might yet be skulking about, Liam had posted extra watches around the manor and the perimeter of the grounds. The women, including Mrs. McGregor, had been warned not to leave the house without an escort until the gunman had been caught.

Kendra paused brushing her hair, then shook her head.

Broden, an earl.

Could it possibly be true?

He'd lost consciousness before anyone had a chance to question him about his astounding declaration. She'd quite forgotten to ask Mrs. McGregor if it was true, and wouldn't it be rude to pry at such a time as this?

A glance at the tabletop clock revealed the hour was a quarter of eleven.

Too agitated and restless to sleep, she quickly plaited her hair, tying the ends with a purple ribbon, and then donned her night robe. She paused at her long bedchamber windows, pushing the heavy emerald velvet aside to stare out over the pastures beyond.

When she'd seen that man sitting there, his gun pointed at Broden, something deep within her, something feral and wild and savage, had burst loose of its confines.

Its foreignness, strength, and ferociousness had frightened and exhilarated her. She could've done that man harm in that instant. Could've killed him for daring to threaten Broden. And she hadn't known she was capable of such dark, violent emotion.

What's more, she couldn't regret it.

After slipping her feet into her slippers, she made for the kitchen for a cup of warm milk laced with brandy, rum, nutmeg, cinnamon, and sugar. Mother called the tasty concoction hot milk punch, and the remedy was a staple in the MacKay household for those suffering from insomnia or a myriad of other elements.

Once in the kitchen, she puttered about, gathering the ingredients to make the hot beverage. Perhaps Mrs. McGregor would enjoy a cup as well. If she were still awake, that was.

Kendra decided she'd make enough for everyone, and what they didn't drink, she'd offer to the servants—a rare treat for them indeed. Twenty minutes later, she climbed the risers, balancing a tray with two steaming cups of the tasty brew.

Carefully picking her way along the corridor, she marveled once more over Broden's astonishing news. He'd claimed he was an English earl. He hadn't received a blow to the head, so there wasn't any reason to doubt him.

Did that mean he'd be leaving the Highlands now?

As a newly titled earl, wouldn't his responsibilities require him to spend a great deal of time—perhaps all of his time now —in England?

She ought to be pleased with the notion. Broden wouldn't be pestering and vexing her.

Pleased was most definitely not the emotion engulfing her. No, indeed.

Why, if she disliked the man so much, did the thought he might leave Scotland cause her heart to plummet and shatter at her feet, like a delicate eggshell-thin teacup?

No immediate, sensible answer sprang to mind.

Outside Broden's bedchamber, she knocked softly.

After a moment, the door swung open to reveal a bleary-eyed and haggard Mrs. McGregor.

"I brought ye a little somethin' to relax ye." Kendra offered an encouraging smile while peering over her shoulder to the bed dominating the chamber. "May I come in and drink mine with ye?"

Mrs. McGregor nodded, gratefully accepting the warm cup. "It smells wonderful," she said as she wearily trudged back to the seat beside the bed where she'd been keeping her vigil. Sinking into the overstuffed armchair, she heaved a sigh before taking a sip. "Och, 'tis wonderful. If I'm no' mistaken, there's a wee nip of spirits mixed in."

"Yer no' mistaken. I made plenty. If ye'd like more, I can easily fetch it for ye." Kendra slipped into the chamber, closing the door quietly behind her. "I've always found milk dosed with spirits and spices verra soothin'. I sleep like a newborn bairn whenever I drink it before bed."

Tonight might prove her a liar, however.

Candles burned on either bedside table, and the hearty fire cast dancing shadows on the open sapphire blue bedcurtains and the coffer and crown decorated ceiling.

She crept nearer the bed, both hands wrapped around her cup. "How is he?"

Seeing Broden, the steady rise and fall of his chest, brought her unexpected reassurance and peace.

Even bandaged and wan, there was no denying he possessed a warrior's powerfully built body. The mounds of his suntanned pectoral muscles, sculpted shoulders, and strong biceps attested to that truth. Curly russet hair, slightly darker than that on his head, covered his chest and the contoured ridges of his abdomen before disappearing beneath the bedding across his waist.

Was he naked?

The idea brought unexpected and uncomfortable heat skittering over her entire body. Of its own volition, her wanton, misguided gaze wandered to the slight lump evident between Broden's legs. She forced her curious attention upward, away from areas she had no wish to speculate about.

Well, not with his mother a few feet away.

His chest hair appeared soft and springy, and Kendra fisted her hand against the urge to splay her fingers in the curls. Was she mad? God would surely punish her for her wanton imagination.

His mother sat right here, the poor woman beside herself with worry, and Kendra's thoughts migrated to carnal urges. She gulped a mouthful of the milk and nearly swore as she scalded her tongue.

Forehead pleated, Mrs. McGregor took another tentative swallow of her milk, her anxious gaze fixed on her son.

"He hasna awoken, but he's no' feverish." Her eyelashes fluttered and her mouth trembled. She was trying so hard to be brave. "I have ye to thank for savin' his life, I'm told. He's all I have left. My only laddie still livin'—"

Her ragged voice caught on a sob, and tears flooded her kind eyes as her face crumpled.

Kendra came swiftly to her side. After placing her cup on the bedside table, she kneeled beside the distraught woman and took Mrs. McGregor's free hand between hers.

"He's a braw, strong man. Too mulish and stubborn to die from a measly little poke to his shoulder. Ye wait and see, Mrs. McGregor, he'll be up, swaggerin' about in nae time."

"I dinna swagger," came a raspy, barely audible male voice.

"Och," cried Mrs. McGregor, swiftly placing her cup on the nightstand and leaning forward to grasp Broden's hand. "Ye gave me a terrible fright, ye did."

She blinked rapidly, trying to dispel the moisture in her eyes as she beamed at him, her love for her son shining on her face.

The dark arcs of his eyelashes fluttered, and he opened his eyes, looking first to his mother and then Kendra. His hooded gaze took in her night robe and the plait draped across her right shoulder.

A flash of awareness zipped across the room, an almost physical connection, yet they weren't touching. Did he feel the current too? The pulsating, magnetic pull?

Utterly implausible. Wholly indescribable.

And, she very much suspected, completely life-altering.

In that instant, the heavens shifted, and her world upended.

Kendra knew, beyond a doubt, that things would never be the same between them.

"Thank ye, Kendra." He lifted his hand, palm upward, reaching for her hand.

She bit her lower lip.

It wasn't appropriate to hold his hand, especially attired only in her night clothing. But he was an invalid, and his mother was present to assure no impropriety.

Sidling around the bed, she pondered this unexpected change in him. Was it simply because he was, quite literally, flat on his back, weak as a newborn calf, and had nearly lost his life?

Or was something else at work here?

No. It must be gratitude. People often behaved differently when direly ill.

She imagined if he'd saved her life, she'd be grateful too.

As she slipped her hand in his, and he curled his fingers around hers, his touch singeing her so that she nearly gasped,

Kendra pondered the warmth and surprising strength. And what was that gleam in his brandy-colored eyes?

"I'm glad ye are recoverin' Broden," she said softly. "Ye've been asleep for hours."

I've been worried about ye.

That she could not say aloud.

His mother finished her milk, her earlier despair having evaporated.

The punch had done its job. *Excellent.*

If only Kendra might've finished her cup, her nerves wouldn't be humming with tension and uncertainty at this moment. She felt wound tighter than a top. Or a corkscrew. Or any number of other things wound around and around until they were tightly coiled.

"Are ye hungry, Broden?" Mrs. McGregor asked as she straightened the perfectly tidy linens, pulling them a trifle higher over the delectable ridges spanning his torso. She, too, must have realized how inappropriate it was for Kendra to see his unclothed state.

"Aye." He still didn't relinquish her hand, even after his mother's pointed look.

Mrs. McGregor's right eyebrow arched high, and her attention fixed on Kendra, giving her a look quite similar to the one *her* mother had given her earlier.

A flush swept her and, for some unfathomable reason, Broden chuckled, then winced and glanced at his bandage.

She very much suspected Broden and his mother shared a secret she wasn't privy to.

FIVE

A fortnight passed, and though it nearly drove him mad, Broden managed to obey the doctor's dictates and his fretting mother's regular pleas to stay abed. What no one knew was that after the fifth day, he began rising when everyone sought their mattresses each night.

Diligent to not open the healing wound, he stretched and conducted a series of calisthenics to keep his muscles strengthened and toned. He refused to become a feeble weakling by the time the doctor finally deemed him recovered enough to leave what was quickly becoming a most hated bed.

It was a wonder anyone ever recovered from ailments if their brains and muscles were always let go to mush.

If it hadn't been for that small amount of exercise and Kendra's company, he might truly have gone mad. Liam visited daily to impart any updates about the manhunt for his shooter, and the Dowager and Lady Penderhaven also put in an appearance each afternoon. But Kendra stayed for an hour or two after breakfast and did likewise in the evenings after dinner.

Her sacrifice rather astounded him, but she claimed that

other than his mother, her schedule allowed the most freedom. Broden would've like to have believed her attentiveness was because she cared at least a little.

Unused to idleness, even when recuperating from something as significant as a gunshot wound, as the fourteenth day dawned, he was dressed in the clothing his mother had thought to bring from home. Everything except for his coat, that was.

Unable to quite wrestle into to the snug-fitting jacket by himself, and not wanting to chance tearing his wound open, he'd opted to forgo the garment. The ladies' sensibilities would have to be offended, for he intended to eat breakfast, wearing only his shirt, belt, and trews.

I bet that never happens in those fancy English houses.

His wound was healing splendidly—the doctor's words, not his—and there were too many things demanding his attention that he couldn't postpone.

Of the shooter, Liam had informed him, they'd found no trace except for horse hoofprints leading to the township. There the trail went frustratingly cold, as any number of people had visited Eddleshaugh that fateful day. Most especially after the locals had been homebound on account of the rains.

Liam had questioned Angus McCurdy and Tobias Moore, the two lodging house owners, and learned Mr. Philibius Oswald had departed the Toadstool Inn and Tavern for London early on the morning of the day the weather cleared.

He'd made his displeasure known far and wide that he'd been unwillingly detained by the Scottish Highland's dismal and most uncooperative clime. He'd also adamantly proclaimed he hoped never to have to venture to the Highlands again.

As Broden had no intention of retaining the man as his attorney, he could think of no reason Oswald would need to.

The other lodgers—three at the Toadstool Inn and four at The Trumpeting Swan—had been unfortunate travelers caught in the storm. Not a soul raised any obvious suspicions amongst the lot.

Still, Broden wanted to speak to the innkeepers himself. He also must travel to his new estate—an ostentatious-sounding place called Sommerley Parke House—to make arrangements for the countess and her children, as well as follow up on his hunch and visit Oswald's offices in London.

And then there was the envious cousin.

Edwin Archibald *Windbag* McGregor

World traveler, investor, and hobnobber with aristocrats. Oh, and until a short while ago, under the misapprehension that *he* would soon be the Fifth Earl of Montforth.

Precisely where had *he* been the day Broden had nearly been picked off?

He meant to find out.

Although he conceded that Edwin might be the sort who hired the job done, rather than commit the act himself. If that were the case, someone knew something, and a few shiny coins had a mysterious way of loosening tongues.

What to do with his mother in his absence was another matter. He was of two minds about her.

He'd be gone at least a fortnight, probably more, and he didn't want her alone at their house until the fiend who shot him was in custody. Yet he was hesitant to impose upon Liam and ask that she be permitted to stay at Eytone Hall until he returned. She'd be safer here.

Independent and proud, she might refuse, in any event.

Perhaps it was best to have a candid discussion with Liam before he made that decision.

Taking one last, disinterested glance in the looking glass above the washstand, he scowled. He'd cut himself shaving. Twice. A scratch on his chin and another nick near his left ear. What was more, his hair hung loose but clean about his shoulders.

Not a ribbon or length of leather was amongst his possessions. His mother's only oversight. Or, perhaps she'd deliberately forgotten to pack them. She'd prefer that he wore his hair shorn short.

His casual appearance would have to do.

No mincing fop here. *Thank God.* A grin split his face as he imagined the reaction of England's perfectly proper and stuffy peers if he should arrive at a grand function appearing as he did at this moment. Nae, wearing a kilt too.

Hell, he might do so, if only to see their responses.

As he exited his chamber, muffled footsteps echoed in the corridor behind him. He turned in the direction of the steady pace, his heart leaping in unanticipated joy.

Kendra, wearing a fetching rich blue gown the color of the sky just before twilight, glided down the passageway, her movements a graceful ballet, tempting and captivating, each swish of her silken skirts a sensual thrum of intrigue enveloped in sheer femininity.

God, but she was devastatingly lovely. Impossibly, amazingly breathtaking. A vision he feasted his eyes upon. He'd like to strip that gown from her fragrant flesh and...

An incandescent smile wreathed her radiant face.

He blinked, almost peering over his shoulder to see the recipient of her smile. It took a handful of breaths to realize the endearing, upward arc was for him. *For him.* What an unforeseen and wholly charming gift.

Edged by full, sable lashes, her wide, gray eyes sparkled. She lightly touched Broden's forearm with her ungloved fingertips. "I'm glad to see ye out of bed, but are ye positive ye are fit enough?" Her focus dropped to his wound and the bandage hidden by his shirt.

Grinning at her concern, and not just a little thrilled by it, he flexed his spine, testing the injury. It pulled uncomfortably and panged with the movement. "Aye, I've had enough of convalescin', thank ye. I do plan to be careful if that alleviates yer worry a mite."

"Hmm." Eyeing his casual attire, she made a noncommittal sound. Her avid attention gravitated down the length of him before she hauled it back to his face. A pinkish flush tinged her cheeks.

Was that womanly appreciation in her searching gaze, the color of quicksilver today?

He quite liked the notion. *Aye, more than liked it.*

"Thank ye once more, Kendra, for sacrificin' yer time and keepin' me company." The truce they'd forced these past two weeks left him on uncertain ground. He unequivocally did not want to return to the verbal sparring and insults, but neither was he certain how to proceed.

He wouldn't define their newly forged relationship as friendship, but he lacked a proper description to define what they'd become.

A delicate blush tinted the graceful slope of her cheeks again. "Ye needna thank me. 'Twas nothin'."

It wasn't nothing. For a wild creature such as Kendra, playing attendance in a sickroom twice daily for a fortnight had been high sacrifice indeed.

After his morning ablutions and he'd broken his fast, she'd read a portion of the news sheet to him. A half dozen times, she'd dined with him too.

In the afternoons, he took a nap, mandated by his fretful mother. Broden didn't argue, for he knew she also took the opportunity to have a lie-down. If he had to pretend to sleep for an hour or two so that she might rest, he'd not grumble. Afterward, before she retired, Kendra read a book to him, or they played chess or cards.

She was damned skilled at the latter two.

Naturally, his mother adopted the role of a chaperone, and more than once he'd caught her evaluating gaze upon him or Kendra while she embroidered or knitted. Did she sense the shift in their relationship? Perceive the burgeoning attraction?

He strove to conceal his interest, but mothers had a way of knowing their children like no other ever could.

More than once, when she'd been alone with him, he'd vow she'd been about to broach the awkward subject. But for some obscure reason known only to her, she changed her mind.

At the first opportunity, Broden must dispel any notions of a match between him and Kendra. He'd seen Mother's eyebrow—her very telling eyebrow—raised several times.

God only knew what she'd contrived in that active and all too creative mind of hers.

Not that he would be opposed to a union with Kendra.

In fact, he couldn't think of anything grander. Two weeks of idleness—mind-numbing idleness and too much time to think—had given him ample time to reflect upon his life. To reflect upon what he wanted for his future, especially now that fate had thrust him into a position of a man of power and means.

A Sassenach earl.

By Odin's teeth, he might've inherited an earldom. But Scotland was now, and would always remain, his home and where he'd live out his life. He wouldn't change who he was as a person simply because he was now encumbered with an earldom, wards, and the role of a most unwilling aristocrat.

He had never desired the ridiculous trappings of a peerage or the restrictions High Society enforced. A simple Scotsman he'd always be.

But several notions—implausible dreams, actually—had tumbled around his mind for years. Notions that had genuine viability now, including establishing a school nearby. Or a home for unfortunate lads and lasses who found themselves on the streets. Mayhap both.

Every child should know how to read and write, no matter their station. But they should also have a roof over their heads, food in their stomachs, and to not live in fear every day.

Shaking off his bitter reflections, Broden extended his elbow to Kendra. "May I escort ye to break yer fast?"

A slightly startled look flashed across her face, but with only the slightest hesitation she placed her fingers into the crook of his arm.

Other than when she'd wrapped her arms around him to keep him atop Sheik, this was the only time he could recall her touching him voluntarily.

They'd never danced together at assemblies or balls. And Broden couldn't help but relish the feel of her hand upon him, her touch once more scorching him, leaving a brand singed upon him. Not to mention sending all sorts of erotic, very unbrotherly thoughts clambering through his mind.

In truth, once she'd bloomed into the striking woman beside him, his thoughts had long since transformed from anything remotely platonic or fraternal.

Wouldn't she spit nails to know his thoughts?

She'd probably clock him with the first thing she could put her hands upon.

Since that first night when he'd awoken to find her standing beside his bed attired only in her nightclothes, her lovely sable hair a thick, plaited rope across her shoulder, and suspecting she was most likely nude beneath the virginal trappings, he'd been unable to dislodge imaginations of her gloriously naked in bed beside him.

It had proved damned awkward with his cock rising to attention and tenting the bedding as his mother puttered around his chamber. Only by focusing on the reason he found himself an invalid in the first place could he wrangle his ardor under control.

Now, as he guided Kendra down the passageway, her honeyed heat, mere inches away, beckoned him. As did her perfume, light and tempting with a promise of spring. Fully aware he flirted with danger and perhaps risked a slap as well, he bent his neck and inhaled deeply.

Her womanly scent tunneled through him, an intoxicating elixir of femininity and Kendra.

She glanced up, curiosity rather than censure in her amused gaze. A winsome smile played around the edges of her soft, plump lips. "Are ye sniffin' me, Broden?"

He chuckled as they turned the corner leading to the top of the stairs. No sense in denying the obvious. "Aye, I am. Ye always smell amazin'."

His superior height gave him a delicious view of the tantalizing hills and valleys her bodice revealed. He was a lecher for taking advantage of it, but damn his eyes if he could haul his attention away from the lush display.

Desperate for a distraction, he said, "Yer fragrance contains lemon?"

Those winged eyebrows of hers that so often pulled together in annoyance and scorn when in his presence, shied skyward as a smile just this side of teasing curved her mouth.

"Are we truly havin' a discussion about my perfume?" A giggle escaped her, and she clapped a palm over her mouth.

He adored her laugh but was rarely gifted the chance to hear it.

"I'm sorry," she said. "I'm no' laughin' at ye. It just seems so ludicrous when, a week ago, I wouldna have believed ye even aware I wore perfume."

Oh, he was aware.

Too damned aware of everything about Kendra MacKay. That was the root of the problem. He couldn't rid his consciousness of her. Even when he wasn't with her.

"Never mind. It isna important." Broden felt a sheer fool. He, who had his choice of any number of women, couldn't hold an intelligent conversation with the only woman that mattered.

Her fingers tightened on his arm minutely, and she said, "If ye must ken, there is lemon in it. And camellia, along with the merest bit of juniper. That gives the fragrance a wee hint of mystery."

"A bit of adventure and sweetness and mystery. And zest," Broden murmured low, finding the conversation oddly arousing.

Did she dab the scent behind those delicate ears? Between her superbly ripe breasts? Inside her shapely elbows? *Elsewhere?*

Lord, help him.

He grew hard at once and closed his eyes for a blink against the tantalizing images springing to mind, as well as the groan bubbling up his throat. "So verra like ye," he managed after what seemed a lust-ridden eternity.

At that ridiculous declaration, her winged, cinder-colored eyebrows rose, and her gaze fairly danced with hilarity. "Are ye positive about the sweetness part?"

They'd reached the stair landing, and he turned her to

him, drawing her minutely nearer. "Och, I'm verra, *verra* sure about the sweetness part."

Then he tipped her chin upward and, uncaring that someone could come upon them at any moment, he brushed her lips with his. God, such an exquisite, scrumptious mouth. And, heaven help him, she tasted as she smelled: sweet and zesty and lemony with a hint of unexplored mystery there as well.

What he wouldn't give to solve the mystery of her body. Over and over and over again.

Instead of jerking away or slapping him or berating him as an opportunistic fiend, she breathed out a ragged sigh and stepped nearer, bracing one hand on his chest and opening her mouth beneath his.

It was glorious. *She* was glorious.

He dipped his tongue into the honeyed cavern, and she tentatively met his stroke. The passion he'd scarcely held in check exploded through him, and all he could think of was pondering her sweet mouth.

Plundering the rest of her.

Making her his.

Taking her in every way possible until he'd stamped himself upon her body, her mind, and her soul for all time. Branding Kendra as his.

She threaded her fingers in his hair, drawing his head closer, arching her neck and leaning into him. Her wondrously bountiful breasts brushed his chest, and a gravelly groan echoed low in his throat.

Christ. Kendra was magnificent.

Temptation and wickedness and utter devastation heralded her delicious-as-sin kisses.

A door snapped closed somewhere nearby, and to protect her from ruination, he forced himself to angle away.

"Anyone might come upon us," he whispered, passion slurring his words.

As if just noticing where they were, how they appeared clinging together like this, she blinked slowly. As if dazed, she glanced up and down the corridor before stepping backward.

"Kendra?"

He wasn't certain what he asked.

Was she all right?

Had he offended her?

Not if her kisses were any indication, he hadn't.

Hands clasped before her, she stared at him, marked uncertainty on her pretty face.

They'd left the bickering and taunting behind.

He could see from the emotions flitting across her features and in her expressive eyes that she knew it as well. And she was just as puzzled as he about what this meant for them.

Where did they go from here?

For years, their interactions had been caustic, tension-filled sniping and insult-hurling interactions. Each trying to best the other with the most sarcastic or cutting rejoinder. Upon reflection, Broden didn't much like himself for his part in their feud.

No other woman had ever been on the receiving end of as much disrespect from him. And here they were at this crossroads. Extraordinarily unforeseen. Tantalizingly trepidatious.

Could she ever desire what he wanted?

A life with her?

He reverently touched her smooth cheek, humbled and thrilled at the impossible softness. Softer than a rose petal. Than down. Than a gossamer web.

Would she be so very wondrously soft everywhere?

Another tidal wave of lust sluiced through him, and he swallowed.

God help him, he yearned to be the man to find out. The only man to ever have the privilege.

He couldn't keep thinking along these perilous lines. Allowing his imagination free rein. Not and go downstairs without someone noticing his obvious arousal.

"Thank ye, Kendra."

Her expression grew more bewildered as if she hadn't come to terms with their kiss and had no idea why he thanked her.

"Thank ye?" she asked. "For what?"

She'd voiced his very thoughts.

He didn't have an answer.

Not one that made any sense.

"There ye are, Broden," his mother called as she advanced toward them, her gait uneven and labored this morning.

Forcing his arousal to recede, he smiled a welcome. He really must acquire a cane for her. She'd refused one thus far, but he feared she might stumble and fall. Particularly at Eytone Hall with its many more stairs than at home.

"Good mornin', my dear," she said when she reached him. She nodded politely at Kendra. "Miss MacKay. I trust ye slept well? Yer gown is most becomin'."

"Thank you. I did indeed rest well," she said, putting a little more distance between herself and Broden.

He hadn't rested well. Not a single night since she'd visited in her night robe and he'd had nothing better to do than conjure one naughty vision after another to occupy his time. It had proved quite diverting and entertaining.

"Please, do call me Kendra, Mrs. McGregor."

Kendra had made that request multiple times, but Mother continued to address her formally.

Why? Because she wanted to keep a barrier of formality between them?

Technically, as an earl's mother, she outranked a feudal baron's sister, so she couldn't use their social positions as an excuse. And he'd never breathed a word of the conflict between him and Kendra.

His mother rarely attended social functions, so she'd not have heard of their less than amiable encounters.

The question would plague him until he had his answer.

"Very well, my dear. Kendra, it is," his mother said.

Broden was fairly certain he gawped like a spectator viewing a freaks of nature exhibition for the first time.

Now his mother agreed?

He knew she suspected his attraction to Kendra. Had she decided to help him court her? It was exactly the sort of thing she would do.

"Good morn, Mother." He found his tongue and greeted her to draw her focus back to him before she noticed Kendra's flushed face and wondered at the reason for her high color.

"I was worried sick when I knocked at yer chamber and ye didna answer." Mother folded her hands to her ample chest in an unconscious, protective gesture. "I was afraid..."

He bent and kissed her rounded cheek. She smelled of lavender water, and vaguely of rum, cinnamon, and nutmeg. Had she been indulging in more of Kendra's hot milk punch?

"I'm sorry. I didna think to let ye ken that I had decided to go down to break my fast this mornin'."

He leaned back, taking in her gown. No apron covered the front. When was the last time he'd seen her without an apron? The holly-berry red and forest-green plaid was one of her finer gowns. Yes, she most definitely was up to something.

Had she noticed Kendra's kiss-reddened, slightly swollen lips?

Only by exercising extreme self-control did he keep from cutting Kendra a sidelong peek.

No. Mother's skeptical eyebrow didn't make a censuring appearance, but a worry-borne crease still balanced on the bridge of her nose. Nevertheless, she summoned a bright smile which included Kendra. "Might I impose upon ye to give me yer arm, Broden?"

At once, he offered his elbow, letting her set the pace as they descended, Kendra following behind.

One hand gripping the banister and the other tightly clinging to his arm, his mother angled her head sideways. "I take it yer leavin' yer sick bed means we'll be departin' today?"

SIX

Departin'?

Kendra stifled her gasp. Or mostly did. A distressed wisp of air escaped her.

Broden glanced over his shoulder, but she couldn't decipher his guarded expression. "No' today."

He faced forward once more, his honey-streaked hair sweeping his broad shoulders. The strands had been soft and surprisingly silky between her fingers. Given his ruggedness, she expected a coarser texture.

"But likely I shall tomorrow," he said. "I'll be gone for at least a fortnight."

"*Ye'll* be gone?" His mother peered up at him, a shadow of disquiet lining her profile.

"Aye." He gave her hand an affectionate pat. "I'd prefer ye to remain here until we find the shooter. I'd worry less about ye and be less distracted, which will make it more difficult for the gunman to venture a second attempt on my life."

Mrs. McGregor made a soft sound in her throat.

Agreement? Annoyance? Apprehension?

Broden was leaving.

Just like that.

As soon as he was able to rise from his sickbed.

Kendra should not be distressed, for pity's sake. In fact, she ought to have expected he meant to leave as soon as he was able. Why she should care, she couldn't say and assuredly wasn't prepared to explore.

A fortnight ago, she'd have danced a jig and whooped for joy. Held the door and given his backside a firm, swift kick to speed him along his way.

The brightness of the winter day now diminished by a shroud of doubt, she followed Broden and his mother into the breakfast room. Only Liam was seated at the table, Mother and Emeline either deciding to take trays in their chambers or choosing to eat later.

Liam rose, a wide smile creasing his face at Broden's presence.

The men clasped hands, letting the action say what they couldn't in words. Why were men so afraid to show affection with each other?

"Ye're lookin' remarkably fit, I must say." Liam resumed his seat and spread his serviette over his lap.

Ever the gentleman, Broden waited for his mother to choose her chair, then pushed it in for her. Kendra took her usual place across the table and, for the first time since she'd been a star-struck adolescent, she wondered if Broden would choose to sit beside her.

Not that she wished him to. She was simply curious. Something had shifted between them, but what precisely? No longer did she consider him her nemesis—an irritating foe to be put in place—but neither was he a friend.

Friends didn't exchange blistering kisses.

Simmons placed a cup of hot chocolate in front of her, and she sent him a grateful smile, inhaling deeply. Nothing like a cup of strong chocolate on a brisk January morning to start the day right. "Thank ye, Simmons. Just toast for me this mornin', please."

The majordomo dipped his regal head, swinging his focus to Mrs. McGregor. "And for ye, Madam?"

"Tea, if ye please, and I confess to bein' quite famished." She sent Broden a maternal look of approval and pride. "My appetite's quite recovered now that I ken ye're well."

Well? Kendra gave a silent snort. He wasn't well. Yes, he could stand upright and dress, but that did not make him *well*.

He was stubborn. Clot-headed. Obstinate. Determined to do what he wanted. Or what he believed needed doing. To forge his own course, just as she determined to define her route through life.

He could still reopen his wound and infection yet presented a risk.

But Kendra also knew a man of Broden's caliber could only bear so much idleness and recuperating. Wisdom decreed he'd wait longer before gallivanting to England.

He'd tell wisdom to bugger herself.

Since when had Broden McGregor heeded anything or anyone but himself? Just a few moments ago, she'd experienced rapture in his arms, carried away on a sea of bliss from his scorching kisses, and now she could easily poke him with her fork.

In a matter of a few short minutes. From bliss to vexation. Euphoria to exasperation.

Mrs. McGregor patted Broden's forearm with her wrinkled hand as he slid deftly into the seat next to his mother.

Kendra staunchly denied the flip of her stomach was anything near disappointment. Naturally, he'd sit next to his mother out of respect for the gentle lady. Taking a seat beside

Kendra would also raise Liam's suspicions since he knew first-hand their aversion to one another.

Her aversion that most definitely appeared to be waning.

Waning?

Women didn't tangle tongues with men they disliked.

"I'd like to speak to the innkeepers today," Broden said as he acknowledged the steaming cup of coffee and plate piled high with food Simmons placed before him with a thankful dip of his strong chin. "Tomorrow, I'm off to Sommerley Parke House to meet the countess and my five wards—"

"Ye have wards?" Kendra exclaimed on an undignified and astonished squeak, jerking her head up to gape.

"Aye. Five lasses rangin' from a month-old infant to a nine-year-old. Their mother is the countess." He wrinkled his forehead. "I dinna ken the wee lasses' names. I imagine all of those details are in the stacks of documents atop my desk."

They'd talked little of his new title while he'd been recuperating. Kendra didn't feel it was her place to pry, and he'd been remarkably closed-mouth about the change in his circumstances.

However, she did have the distinct impression he wasn't altogether keen on being the newest Earl of Montforth. Evidently, the title came with more than an honorific, lands, and wealth.

Five wards.

And a countess. Dinna forget the countess.

Just how old was this countess? Was she beautiful? Refined?

No doubt.

Finding that train of thought troubling, Kendra switched to another.

She'd never imagined Broden in the role of a father, let alone a guardian—to five small girls.

To her knowledge, he hadn't been around children all that much. Heaven help his wards if one or two or all became enamored of him. God only knew what he might say or do to scar their little souls to discourage their infatuation.

Unfair, her conscience chided.

He'd been deep into his cups the night she'd eavesdropped on him. To hold something against him that had occurred years before, something he had no knowledge he'd done, wasn't just. Nor was it mature or healthy.

Kendra had accepted those truths years ago. Had known she needed to let the childishness go. She was an adult. Far past time she put her injured pride to rest. But every time she intended to act upon that wisdom, he'd done something to incense her again.

Mrs. McGregor stirred her tea, the lace cap covering her gray-peppered hair fluttering slightly at her movement.

Kendra couldn't help but like the Scotswoman. Her devotion to her son was endearing, and she'd gone out of her way not to be an imposition during her stay. Nary a cross word had come from her mouth, which curved upward increasingly as her son's health improved.

She and Mother had spent several hours together knitting in the rose salon while Broden napped in the afternoons, the times Mrs. McGregor had declined to take a rest herself. The orphans in the foundling home would all have new caps this winter thanks to the two ladies' busy hands.

"I must say, I never expected the day would come that any son of mine would inherit the earldom." Mrs. McGregor sliced a glance at Liam as she raised her teacup. Her attention slid to Kendra over the cup's rim.

"I dare say none of us could've predicted such a thing," Liam said politely, before directing a wry grin at Broden.

"We've quite a convoluted family tree," she said, inspecting the plate of food before her. "Branches stickin' out in every which direction. Quite a prolific family too." Squinting, she aimed her regard upward in contemplation. "If I recall correctly, Broden inherited the title from the line of his great-great-grandfather's youngest brother."

Broden turned to look at her, his hawkish brows knitting together. "Ye kent I was in line to inherit?"

Picking up her fork, she gave a little offhand shrug of one plump shoulder. "I kent a remote possibility existed, but I truly didna expect it. After all, Standish was a younger son. And his father was a younger son. I tell ye," she said, waving the eating utensil, "that family has had a wicked run of bad luck in the past decade."

Broden wasn't a younger son.

But he was one of three, and his brothers were both dead —the younger to a fever when a wee laddie, and the other to a tragic accident when he'd fallen from a tree just shy of his eighth birthday.

Even as Mrs. McGregor said the words, her countenance fell, a somber shadow marring her earlier animation. "And now some villain is intent on doin' ye harm. My only remainin' son and kin."

Broden covered her hand with his and gave her one of his winsome, comforting don't-worry-I'll-make-everything-right smiles. "Dinna repine on it. The previous earls had the misfortune of livin' in England. I intend to live out my days in Scotland until I'm a feeble old codger, bowed over, toothless, and bald."

"There's a lovely image," Liam quipped.

Kendra couldn't summon the same jollity. In fact, the oddest despondency flooded her.

Broden playfully chucked his mother's chubby chin. "But I think I shall purchase a larger house, so ye better start plannin' the furnishin' and how many servants ye wish to hire. I've often admired Glenawayshire, and the estate 'tis no' only available for purchase, 'tis also but a scant five miles away."

His mother's calm pale-brown eyes lit with excitement. "Glenawayshire? My, that 'tis impressive. A right proper house for an earl."

Again, Mrs. McGregor cast Kendra a surreptitious look, but she pretended absorption in her—ah—toast. Yes, the bread browned to perfection.

A wife generally saw to the furnishing of a house and hiring of the staff. Broden had no plans of wedding soon then. Not even for an heir, now that he bore the burden of continuing the line?

Or perhaps, he didn't plan to wed yet. Mayhap, Broden needed time to put his affairs in order and become accustomed to his new role. She couldn't find fault with that logic if that were the case.

Kendra had only been to Glenawayshire once, three years ago, before the previous owners—Sassenachs—had decided the Highlands were too rusticated for their refined tastes.

More palatial than manor-like, the mansion boasted sixteen bedrooms. He'd need to find a countess and get busy if he intended to fill them all with wee McGregor bairns.

Or would the children be Montforths?

Liam focused his attention on his sausage. After stabbing a piece with his fork, he leveled Broden a considering look. "I ken ye dinna need my advice, but I dinna think 'tis wise for ye to travel alone."

Kendra agreed wholeheartedly.

And so, apparently, did Mrs. McGregor, from the relieved expression washing over her face.

Broden gave a slow, reflective nod.

Kendra released the breath she'd held in anticipation of his answer and whether his typical obstinacy would rear its head.

"Aye. I wanted to discuss that with ye," he said. "If it wouldna be too much of an imposition, I'd like ye, the Kennedy brothers, Roxdale, and McPherson to accompany me. I'd ask Catherwood, but he's still honeymoonin'." He angled his knife, the tip covered with preserves. "Mayhap even Wallace and Rutherford, if their wives dinna object."

Most of the Scots he'd just named had foiled a plot to assassinate Emeline last autumn. The men trusted each other completely, much as brothers would.

Liam narrowed his eyes reflectively as he chewed. He swallowed, then took a sip of his coffee. "Aye. I think there's wisdom in travelin' in numbers, but no' so many that ye draw undue attention. I'd say ye, me, and two more at the most."

The whole while they spoke, her agitation high, Kendra attended to her breakfast. She spread preserves over a slice of toast and took a bite. The food had no flavor. No texture. She might've been eating foolscap.

She couldn't stop thinking of how many of the former Earls of Montforth had died premature deaths. Now Broden was the new earl, and some fiend had already tried to kill him.

Coincidence?

Perhaps. Perhaps not.

Who was she trying to fool? Most likely, not a coincidence at all.

Broden brought his regard to her across the table, and their gazes tangled.

She wouldn't plead for him not to go.

Not only wasn't it her place, she understood he must leave. He'd never shirked responsibilities, and although he mightn't want the duties and obligations that accompanied the earldom, he'd do what needed doing.

Besides, until she had analyzed whatever *this* was that she felt for him now—well, her thoughts and emotions were a messy, gnarled confusing knot. And it might take some time to pick the threads apart and sort them all out. To identify whatever had her in a jumbled snarl.

He'd kissed her. And she'd kissed him back. And it had been divine. Something, for certain, she'd never expected in a lifetime.

She still tingled at the strength of his corded muscles as he'd held her in his arms. She'd pressed her palm and breasts against the granite wall of his chest and reveled in it. The man was all sinewy muscle, strong angles and lines. Primal masculine virility ready to burst loose and devour.

God help her, she wanted—yearned—to be devoured by him.

He'd smelled of soap and clean linen and Broden.

Masculine, the merest bit musky, with a hint of cloves and bay.

She still couldn't rid her mind of the vision of his scrumptiously naked chest and the mesmerizing light brown hair covering the even ridges marching along his hard-hewn torso. Oh, how she wanted to touch that delectable flesh. Run her fingertips along the rigid planes. Fan her palm on or rub her nose in the tempting hair on his chest.

Good Lord.

How could she have gone from reviling him to admiring his physique like a lusty, experienced tavern wench?

Her nape hairs tingled, and Kendra glanced upward through her lashes.

Yes, he watched her. His rich brown eyes trained on her mouth.

He recalled their stolen kiss too.

Was he as bewildered as she? As much at a loss to understand the unexpected magnetism escalating between them?

She took a sip of her chocolate, needing to steady her unruly pulse and irregular breathing. This new manner in which Broden upset her world was even more disturbing than when he'd continually miffed her.

A most unpleasant thought burrowed its nasty way into her mind.

God above.

Was she back to being the silly, besotted girl that she'd been years ago?

Remembered humiliation suffused her, and only with a supreme force of will did she keep her face impassive.

Nae, I willna make the same mistake again.

Wear her heart on her sleeve.

She mightn't have a great deal of experience with men and kissing—none, except for him, truth to tell—but she was female enough to recognize Broden's arousal. Quite amorous arousal if the hard length nudging her belly while they kissed was any indication.

But did he desire *her*?

Or would any woman do?

SEVEN

Broden did indeed speak to the two hostelries. Much to his disappointment, he learned nothing more than Liam had during his inquires. He'd even queried at the livery stable and the three other pubs in Eddleshaugh.

No one had noticed anyone unusual lurking about. Except for Oswald, that was. The lanky solicitor was hard to miss. His contempt for the locals had been palatable and earned him no kind words or warm recommendations after his departure.

If only Broden knew what his long lost cousin several times removed, Edwin Archibald Wiggins McGregor, looked like. He could've then described the man he was fairly certain had attempted to kill him.

Except, as he'd reflected earlier, Edwin may have hired someone to do the job.

Likely had done so, and that made tracing the cutthroat much more difficult. Impossible, in truth.

Broden, Liam, Camden Kennedy, and Bryston McPherson were to leave in two days for Sommerley Parke House. Broden bristled at the delay, but the other men needed time to prepare for their absences. Keane, the Duke of

Roxdale, conveniently had business in England and had made arrangements to meet Broden in London.

Roxdale knew his way around the city and was acquainted with several members of Society as well. And he'd promised to introduce Broden to their elite circles.

He'd rather be lashed.

A missive was sent ahead, notifying the Countess of Montforth of his pending arrival. That was what he'd been about the day someone had tried to kill him—posting the letter. But considering how irregular the post was, he wouldn't be surprised if she weren't aware of his coming until he stood at the door surrounded by his Scots friends.

Hmm, that might send the unsuspecting woman into a swoon.

As he strode the path from the stables after relinquishing Sheik to the stable boy, he contemplated his future. The earldom had plunged him from the comfortable, uncomplicated life he'd enjoyed into something quite foreign. Unwelcome.

He felt slightly adrift.

His mother didn't seem affected one way or the other about their newly elevated station and, to his relief, she'd acquiesced to remain at Eytone Hall in his absence. The Dowager Baroness Penderhaven had eagerly agreed to lend her expertise in suggestions about furnishings and servants. Liam's man of business had conceded to make an offer for Glenawayshire too.

At least Mother would have something to occupy her time while he was away, and perhaps she wouldn't fret overly much.

The women had even summoned the local seamstresses to begin working on a new wardrobe for her. Nothing too elaborate, she'd insisted. Liam had suggested Broden visit a tailor while in London as well.

He supposed his position required a few of the fancier togs men of his rank wore, but by God, nothing with ruffles, lace, or in colors more fitting for tropical birds or stage actresses with questionable reputations.

He'd just rounded the corner beside the tidy hedgerow when Kendra exited the rear of the house, her hood pulled over her hair. Carrying a basket, she moved swiftly with purpose, and it only took him a moment to realize she was headed to the stables by way of another pathway.

Before he left for Sommerley Parke House, he must speak to her about their kiss.

A fortnight or more was too long to wait to have the discussion. Honestly, Broden wasn't sure what to say. It shouldn't have happened. But it had, and now he must decide what to do about it. Ignoring their embrace wasn't an option. Doing so could very well create a bigger chasm between them than what had been there before.

His raging desire for Kendra had grown every time he saw her in recent months, but until he'd inherited the earldom and she'd kissed him so eagerly, he'd never seriously considered a union between them. But now…?

It wasn't just her beauty that drew him. Though her brilliant gray eyes in a diamond-shaped face, a nose as impertinent as she was, a small pointed chin just as stubborn too, and skin so pearly smooth—he'd wondered more than once if she used cosmetics—left him breathless more often than he'd care to admit.

Neither was it her effervescent wit, lively conversation, or a figure so lush and delectably formed that he kept his hands balled a great deal of the time when around her to resist reaching out and testing the curves of her flesh. Yes, each attribute contributed to her allure, but that didn't—*couldn't*—explain his obsession with her.

The appeal, he'd decided while laying sleepless again last night, was the whole of her, each a piece of a perfectly constructed puzzle. Incomplete without all the other unique pieces, but, when assembled, brilliant and breathtaking beyond compare.

As yet, there'd been no opportunity for a private conversation. Although she didn't deliberately avoid him as she'd done in the past, he couldn't help but notice that neither did she allow them to be alone.

Did she fear he'd try to kiss her again?

Hell, *he* was afraid he would.

No, he *knew* he would.

Reversing his steps, Broden aimed for the opposite side where the boxwood hedge opened onto the expansive, rolling greens. Kendra emerged from behind the shrubberies, and he increased his pace.

"Kendra," he called. "Please wait."

For a long stretch, she stood still, tense and quivering, like a startled deer poised to flee.

Finally, she turned toward him, lifting her hood a few inches. A small, puzzled furrow wrinkling her forehead, she waited for him to approach and offered a tentative smile. "How fared yer trip to Eddleshaugh? Any good news?"

"Nae." Broden shook his head, slightly distracted by her hesitancy. "Nothin' that we didna already ken." He eyed her basket, partially filled with apples. "What are ye doin' with those?"

She glanced downward before lifting the forearm the hamper was slung over a couple of inches. "These are the rest of last years' that were stored in the root cellar. Cook's directed the removal of the old produce, so I'm takin' them to the horses. They'll enjoy the treat, even if they arena quite as crisp as fresh fruit."

Reaching back into his mind, he couldn't recall a time Kendra hadn't adored horses.

A vision of her atop a stout, pewter-colored Shetland pony sprang to mind. Her hair in braids, she'd trotted the docile beastie around the paddock, a broad grin wreathing her round face and exposing her missing front teeth.

She couldn't have been more than six or seven.

"Look, Broden," she'd called, laughing in the unconstrained and exuberant way only children do. "I'm ridin' Shadow all by myself." She'd been so proud and confident. So excited to share her accomplishment.

Eager to join Liam and Quinn on an excursion to The Crowing Cockerel, he'd scarcely spared her an impatient half-smile and an even shorter wave. In truth, it had been the new owner of the pub's curvaceous and very, *very* amiable daughter they'd been eager to ogle.

Kendra's glowing countenance had fallen, and she'd bitten her lower lip before flinging those long braids over her shoulders in offense and trotting the pudgy pony in the opposite direction.

As if it had been yesterday, he recalled her crestfallen expression, swiftly followed by proud indifference. How many times had he treated her so offhandedly? Disregarded her? Made her feel unimportant?

Something akin to shame sluiced through him.

He'd do better by his wards. He must. The responsibility weighed heavily upon him.

They mightn't know him, but he was now accountable for their wellbeing, and they'd not be neglected or feel unwanted. He hadn't worked out the details regarding precisely what that meant. Meeting them would likely help him formulate a plan.

Another incident with Kendra flared to memory.

Why now?

Perchance because he couldn't deny he hadn't been kind to her over the years?

She'd been fourteen or fifteen—a lonely girl with no females of her age living nearby to play or socialize with. For nearly seven years, she'd tagged after him and Liam, and he had grown heartily exasperated with her constant shadowing.

He'd spied her hiding in the hayloft, silently staring at him —her somber eyes, big silvery pools—as he and Liam saddled their horses.

Leaving her behind once again.

When Liam had led his mount outside, Broden had craned his neck to look at her peeping less than subtly down from her perch.

"Dinna ye have a doll to play with? Sewin' to do? A kitten to occupy ye?" He'd scowled as he swiped his too-long hair back, then swept a hand down his horse's withers to calm the high-spirited beast.

"I dinna like playin' with dolls. 'Tis borin," she snapped, highly affronted. Several pieces of straw stuck from her rich, chocolatey-brown hair, laying in wild curls and tangles about her shoulders that day.

"Well, ye need to find somethin' fittin' for a young lady to do and stop pesterin' yer brother and me." Hell, he'd been an arrogant, insensitive ass. "We're adults, and yer a child. Ye need to leave us be."

His chest constricted at the memory of his callous words. His heartless disregard for Kendra's feelings. Her loneliness.

Her gorgeous eyes flashing with frustration and wounded anger, she'd jerked her mutinous chin upward. Even from where he'd stood below, he clearly saw the tears sparkling on her lashes.

"I vow the day will come, Broden McGregor, ye mean, conceited *arse*, when I'll be the one tellin' ye to leave *me* alone," she said, her voice quaking as she sniffled and angrily swiped at the tears on her plump cheeks. "Just see if it disna."

"In yer dreams, lass." He'd laughed heartily and left the barn, not once looking back.

Now here he was, all these years later, feeling rather like a pest himself. Her very prediction had come to fruition. "May I walk with ye?"

Head tilted, she studied him. Running that too astute, inquisitive gaze that was so Kendra over him. "But werena ye headed toward the house?"

So, she *had* seen him and chosen to pretend she hadn't. Still, she hadn't retreated. He could count that as an improvement.

"I was," he admitted. "To speak to ye."

"Why?"

It was his turn to regard her with a degree of bewilderment.

She hadn't even attempted delicacy.

"I think ye ken why, *leannan*."

After a swift glance around the opening, he cupped her elbow and guided her to the hedge's protective shadows. They were suitably hidden from the house behind the six foot-high, neatly trimmed boxwood. From this angle, they were not visible from the stables either.

She surprised him by sighing deeply. Her attention swerved to somewhere over his shoulder. "If this is about the kiss, ye needna fret. I ken ye are a man of—*ah*—strong needs, and I'm the only unattached female—"

Jesus on the blessed cross.

Did she think he'd only kissed her because she was the only lass available?

Was her opinion of him truly so low?

"Hold there, Kendra." He cupped her delicate shoulders,

forcing her to face him. "Do ye ken how insultin' yer sugges-tion is that I kissed ye because ye were the only accessible woman around? I thanked ye for honorin' me with yer kiss because it meant somethin' to me. I hope it did to ye as well."

Her bosom rose as she drew in a deep breath, and he damned himself for being unable to drag his attention away.

He'd always been a breast man.

Some men were leg men. Some adored a plump bum, and while he certainly could appreciate a shapely calf and thigh or a delectable, pear-shaped bottom, breasts... Ah, glorious breasts. Those magnificent, impossibly soft, yet firm rounded mounds made for kissing, licking, and fondling.

And none compared to the swell of Kendra's ivory breasts. *Och hell*. His loins responded with predictable enthusiasm.

Broden swallowed and forced himself to think of some-thing—*anything*—else.

The earldom. Mother. My wards. The hole healin' in my chest.

"Ye do have a rather—erm—*colorful* reputation, Broden. I'm nae fool. Ye dinna suddenly find yerself enamored of me." She adjusted the basket before meeting his gaze boldly. "We shared an enjoyable kiss. Let's leave it at that. I expect nothin' from ye, and ye shouldna expect anythin' from me either."

She made to move away, but he caught her elbow.

"'Twas more than that, love."

Her eyes flashed, the blue and gold flecks in her irises sparking.

In surprise? Anger? Excitement?

"Was it?" She narrowed her gaze to shrewd, pewter slits. "How precisely? We've been at odds for years. *Years*, Broden! One kiss disna change that." She waved an ungloved hand, the fingertips slightly pink from the cold. "Blame my participation on relief that ye're recoverin'. That the dastard who shot ye didna succeed. To a wild, impetuous whim."

"Ye dinna believe that any more than I do," he said, surprised by the vehement emotion compelling his words.

Did she?

Her reaction suggested it meant far more.

But why this retreat?

Why this obvious effort to downplay what had happened?

She made to step around him, but he gently caught her free hand.

Her attention on his hand gripping hers, she murmured softly, "Broden, there are a dozen or more reasons for our impulsiveness, and neither of us needs to make more of the situation than what it was."

"What are ye afraid of, lass?" Broden needed to know. To understand.

The connection had been real. Vibrant. Powerful. He was experienced enough to know what had passed between them wasn't commonplace.

However, she wasn't.

This phenomenon wasn't something he'd readily relinquish either.

She opened her mouth, her gaze softening for the briefest moment before her lashes dipped, blocking her eyes—her secrets—from his view.

"Trust me, Kendra."

Her eyelids flew open, and she shook her head. "I canna."

"Why no'?"

It was his turn to be blunt.

Her chest rose and fell again as if she struggled to remain calm. At last, she looked at Broden squarely.

"Ye once said I was a splotchy-faced dumplin' with perpetually knotted hair and grubby smudges on my chubby cheeks.

Yer dislike and disdain for me extends back many years. I canna believe one passionate kiss erases years of yer contempt."

Jerking his head up, Broden narrowed his eyes, not recalling ever having said anything so harsh. "I never did. That would've been cruel. I'd never have been deliberately unkind to ye."

Even in their verbal sparring, he'd never crossed the line into insulting. He'd been stern. Mocking. Sarcastic. Disdainful.

Hell. Weren't they all part of the same verbal, mean-spirited arsenal?

Had he truly been belittling and disparaging her, inflicting wound after wound, and not even realized his culpability? That made him the worst sort of sod. An insensitive clodpoll.

An eyebrow winged upward, and a pained expression pinched Kendra's pale face. A hint of embarrassment shone in her eyes until she averted her gaze. "Ye also said..." She sucked in a wobbly breath and two bright spots appeared on her cheeks. "Ye said, ye'd never kent a lass who ate more sweets, and ye felt sorry for my horse."

"I..."

Shite.

What could he say to that?

He raked a hand through his hair. "God," he groaned, despising his younger, self-absorbed self. Had he ever said something so callous? Aye, she wouldn't lie about something so humiliating. "That's beyond contemptible. I have nae memory of sayin' such things, but I beg yer pardon, nonetheless."

"Ye were in yer cups." She shot a gaze over the hedgerow to the house. "In the library with Liam and a bottle of whisky. Ye drank a lot back then."

Och, hell.

As a stupid, callow youth, angry about his father's death the year he'd turned one and twenty, he'd indulged in strong spirits way too often to obliterate the gruesome memory of finding him beaten nearly to death during a robbery in Edinburgh. He'd died in Broden's arms, and he'd exacted brutal revenge on the men responsible.

A large man, even then, Broden had attacked the thieves. They were no match for his superior size and strength. Or his grief-borne rage. He'd broken their necks. Snapped them like twigs from a tree.

An act he wasn't proud of but couldn't entirely repent of either.

It was devastation on the dirty face of one of the men's sons that still haunted him. The wee lad had tried to protect his father, just as Broden had protected his. A couple of months later, when a degree of reason had returned and gut-wrenching remorse had overcome him, he'd tried to find the lad and his family, if he'd had any.

He'd wanted to apologize and offer to help them financially. Even after searching for a fortnight, he'd had no luck. To this day, he wondered what had happened to the wee, skinny lad and remorse gnawed at his peace of mind.

That guilt had also driven him to the bottle.

When pished, he couldn't remember much the next day, which was one reason that he never drank to excess anymore. More than once, he'd awoken in a strange woman's bed, with no memory how he'd come to be there.

What had been a sliver of shame had expanded into full-blown self-disgust.

Kendra didn't much like the Broden McGregor she already knew. She'd be appalled and repulsed if she knew him for the former womanizing drunkard who'd killed two men.

"I'm nae holdin' a grudge if that's what yer thinkin'," she

said. "It has been many years, but I canna help but think what a man says while pickled comes straight from his heart."

Her assumption wasn't farfetched.

"I *was* plump, and I had hideous red spots all over my face. I didna care much about my appearance back then. But ye see, Broden, I worshipped ye as only a silly, young lass can. Ye wounded me with yer careless words. Wounded my spirit, and it took me a long while to overcome that hurt."

"Kendra...?" He clamped his teeth together, despising the self-centered arse who'd hurt her so long ago. "If ye say I said those untenable things, I dinna doubt ye. I shallna insult ye by offerin' pitiful excuses. I was an inconsiderate, unforgivable blackguard."

A fragile smile softened the corners of her mouth. "'Tis a long time ago. I shallna deny it stung, but I've tried to put it behind me. Still, until two weeks ago, ye still treated me like I had the plague."

Because he'd been so bloody frustrated at her rejection of him. Her enmity. Now he understood why she'd rebuffed him at every turn.

"I can only beg for yer forgiveness." He captured her hand again. Somehow, he must right the wrong he'd done. That she'd suffered from for so long. "Tell me what I must do to make it right?"

She tilted her head sideways as if confused by or uncertain of his motives. "Perhaps..." A long, uncertain paused stretched out between them before she dampened her lower lip. "Perhaps, we could start over?"

EIGHT

Start over?

Kendra had just blurted the first thing that had sprung to mind. A clever idea, if she didn't say so herself. Slightly terrifying too, if she were completely honest with herself.

Was it possible to start over?

Really, truly start over? Expunge their past, and begin fresh and new?

It astonished her how much she'd like to try.

"Aye, lass. Let's start over." Honesty in his gaze, a delighted grin split Broden's face. He bent into an exaggerated, flourishing bow, and she smothered a giggle.

Never had she seen him this jovial or charming.

"My lady, I am Broden McGregor, the newly titled Earl of Montforth." He waggled his eyebrows in a cocky, confident manner. Speaking like the stuffiest lords she encountered in Edinburgh, he droned, "Yer humble and most devoted servant."

"Humble *and* devoted?" Unchecked laughter made her voice uneven.

She quite liked this carefree scamp.

She gripped her cloak and skirts, rather awkwardly given the basket she still held, and sank into a deep curtsy, as embellished as his bow had been.

"My lord. 'Tis a pleasure to make yer acquaintance."

She batted her eyelashes while gazing up in what, she hoped, was a coquettish manner. It felt rather like she'd a bit of dust in her eye and was trying to rid herself of the annoyance.

"I am Kendra MacKay, sister to Baron Penderhaven." As she rose, she made a sweeping gesture. "The owner of this fine estate upon whose grounds we stand. Och, and alas, I am merely Miss MacKay. No' 'my lady.'"

"We'll see," he said, his voice gone deep and suggestive.

A thrill similar to what she'd experienced when his mouth had ravaged hers so wonderfully this morning skittered across her shoulders.

Did he imply what she thought he did?

That he genuinely was considering making her his countess?

The notion was so far gone that she could scarcely frame the idea in her mind. Broden hadn't said as much, not directly. She'd best temper any giddy responses lest he misinterpret and make a bigger fool of herself.

The delight, the anticipation, the optimism competing for dominance were secondary to the relief tunneling through her veins. Skipping happily along her spine too. She'd taken a monumental gamble, and the risk had paid off amazingly.

So far.

She'd been given a second chance to win the affections of Broden McGregor, and, by God, she wasn't going to botch the opportunity. The past offenses and hurts she'd stuff into a chest, then lock and pack them way in a dank dungeon where they'd stay forever. Never to discourage her with their unwanted presence again.

Neither ignorant nor in denial, Kendra knew full well his reputation with the lasses.

Once, when he'd been particularly odious to her, she'd complained to Liam that Broden wasn't fit company, hoping her brother would, at the very least, banish him from their home. Liam had tolerantly assured her that much of what was said about Broden McGregor was exaggerated. In some instances, pure fabrications.

Liam had continued to encourage her and Broden to make amends. He wanted them to form an accord. How could he not? They were two of the people he most loved in the world, and, as he'd told her one time, it dismayed him to see them constantly at odds.

Admiring Liam for his loyalty was one thing, but he'd been most adamant about Broden's roguish reputation. According to Liam, Broden was not a philanderer. She hadn't been convinced, and, at the time, had said as much too. Nevertheless, she'd been forced to concede he mightn't be the womanizing libertine she'd painted him in her mind.

Not that Broden was a saint by any stretch of a maiden's imagination. But if he were truly improper company, Liam wouldn't have given him leave to spend so much time at Eytone Hall.

Her brother's defense of Broden was heartfelt and sincere, and she began to understand his faith in the man.

Wasn't she doing the same thing now?

Putting her faith in Broden?

Trusting that whatever *this* thing budding between her and Broden, it was worth pursuing?

"Does this mean ye intend to formally court me, Broden?"

Today was Kendra's day for boldness, it seemed.

That mischievous twinkle appeared in his rich whisky-tinted eyes that she so adored. A more intent glint, hinting at a secret promise, gleamed there too. "Aye, lass. I'll need to speak with yer brother first. I'd no' have his displeasure aimed toward me for oversteppin'."

Liam would approve.

Broden was his best friend, and if Kendra was willing to accept Broden's attention, she could fathom no reason Liam would object. Other than he'd be dumbfounded at the request. Possibly think they'd both taken complete leave of their senses. Or that Broden was making a May game of him and playing him for a clodhead or a numpty fool.

He'd believe every one of *those* reasons before he accepted Broden had a romantic interest in Kendra. Mayhap, it would be wise for her to be present when Broden spoke to her brother.

Yes, that was the best course.

She passed Broden the basket of apples. "Why dinna ye accompany me to the stables, and after we give the horses the apples, we can have a word with Liam?"

"*We*?" Skepticism skated over Broden's lean face.

"Aye. I fear Liam will no' believe ye unless I give my assurances that I desire yer attentions." A flush warmed her from waist to hairline at the declaration.

A rather smug, definitely primal, male expression descended onto Broden's features, but he only said, "Aye. I'd like to have the matter settled before I leave for England."

Kendra's chest cramped, reality tempering her newfound happiness.

Broden would leave tomorrow—to plunge headlong into the life of an English aristocrat. He'd now have opportunities and access to powerful people beyond anything he might've conceived. His life would never be the same.

How could it?

What if... What if he found that he preferred that privileged life?

If he preferred his English estate? Needed a delicate, refined English rose as his countess?

She gave herself a firm mental shake and silent scold.

No, the Broden McGregor she knew was a Highlander through and through. Scotland was in his very bones. While they had locked horns many times over the years and gone toe-to-toe with their verbal sparring, she'd never once known him to be a man who didn't keep his word.

As they strode the path to the stables, he tucked her hand into the crook of his elbow. She quite liked how comfortable and natural the gesture was.

Little whiffs of his soap and cologne wafted to her.

Had he always smelled this divine?

A cow mooed, and another answered. The cattle's thick, shaggy coats protected them from the Highland's harsh winters. One of Kendra's favorite things to do was to visit the newborn calves in late spring, their impossibly big brown eyes so sweet and trusting.

Lifting her face to the sky, enjoying the feeble rays of sunshine valiantly shining through the smattering of clouds, she narrowed her eyes. The day had started well enough, but the ominous clouds gathering on the horizon portended more rain.

Perhaps even snow, given how cold it had become the past two days.

She could only hope the weather wasn't too unforgiving, for Broden and the others departed in the morn. No matter what. Traveling in the rain was miserable enough, but in snowfall, nigh onto hellish.

They entered the stables, the comforting scents of warm

horseflesh, hay, oats, and liniments filling the cozy atmosphere. As a child, she'd spent a great deal of time playing in the haylofts, often spying on Liam, Broden, and Quinn.

Sheik poked his great head over his box and whickered for Broden.

"I just rode ye," Broden said, the smile in his voice belying any reproach. "Ye canna miss me that much already."

Jack, the stable lad, cut a glance toward them from the box he mucked out. "He's right fond of ye, he is, sir."

"I think 'tis sweet," Kendra said.

Not to be outdone, Pandora's creamy head appeared over her gate. "Hello, my lovely," Kendra crooned, offering the gentle mare an apple. Pandora greedily accepted her treat as Broden offered a fruit to Sheik.

Sensing they were missing out, several more horses hurried to see what the commotion was about. In a few short breaths, nearly every box had an expectant equine seeking an apple.

Kendra laughed and passed the basket to Jack. "There should be enough for them to each have one."

He accepted the hamper, a wide grin of anticipation curving his mouth. "I'll return the basket to the house when I'm done, Miss Kendra."

"Thank ye," she said, giving Pandora one last stroke down her smooth her neck. "We'll go for a nice long ride soon, my sweet." If only around the paddock and stables.

She hadn't been permitted to ride since Broden's shooting, and Pandora didn't understand why she wasn't being saddled when Kendra was in the barn.

Turning, she met Broden's speaking gaze, her anticipation sending little tendrils of heat sneaking up her face. This was new territory for her. She wasn't nervous, exactly, but her typical confidence had momentarily deserted her.

One hand extended toward the open stable doors, he

flashed a knowing smile. Obviously, his confidence hadn't been affected one iota. *Men.*

"Shall we?" The upward turn of his mouth, as well as the invitation his proffered hand offered, were irresistible.

Well, to someone who had no desire to resist them, they were. "Aye."

Knowing full well Jack and the other groomsmen, trainers, and stable hands likely watched their every move, Kendra was mindful to keep her demeanor polite but reserved while regarding Broden.

A chuckle escaped her once they'd made good their escape, and they weren't in danger of being overheard.

He cocked an eyebrow over his sinfully handsome face. "What, may I ask, do ye find so funny?"

"Surely ye saw the baffled looks on their faces, and the puzzled glances the poor stable hands kept sendin' each other. We've never spent that long in one another's company without squabblin'. They dinna ken what to make of it." Giggling again, she glanced behind her. "'Tis as if they were waitin' for the other boot to drop."

His rich chuckle mixed with hers as he boldly seized her hand and whisked her into a copse of trees between the house and barns. "I wonder what they'd say if they kent I want to make ye my countess?"

Kendra went utterly still, peering up at him, her heart fluttering like a trapped wren in her chest. She'd been correct about his innuendo earlier then. "Isna it awfully premature to be thinkin' along those lines? For years, we've scarcely been civil to one another."

But hadn't there always been an undercurrent of sexual awareness between them?

For certain, she'd been very conscious he was a virile man, and when she'd disliked him, it had infuriated her to no end that she could countenance such irrational stirrings toward him.

Did Broden feel the same way?

Had he been as conflicted?

Had he experienced the same maddening internal battle?

"Aye, 'tis early to be comtemplatin' such a drastic step, but I want ye to have nae doubts my intentions are honorable." He gathered her hands in his, brushing his thumbs across the knuckles in a steady, mesmerizing caress. "We've chosen to put our past differences behind us to give us the possibility of a future together."

He drew her near, and she didn't object. Not if it meant more of those soul-searing kisses. Besides, she agreed with his assessment. The past was behind them. She wanted, above all else, to look to the future. *Their* future.

Standing up on her tiptoes, she wended her arms around his sturdy neck, relishing the low rumbling growl throttling up his throat a mere second before his mouth found hers.

"Well, I'll settle for more kisses for now," she murmured against his warm, firm mouth. "Let's just wait and see what tomorrow brings."

"I willna be here tomorrow, *leannan*."

God, he wouldna.

And she didn't know for certain when he'd return. Never before had she regretted his departure. Now the thought brought stinging tears to her eyes. She closed her eyelids to hide her dismay.

He kissed her nose. "I adore yer nose. Do ye ken that?"

Laughter bubbled upward from behind her ribs, and she opened her eyes, his absurdness restoring her good-humor. "My nose." She touched the appendage, brushing her forefinger down its length. "It has a hideous hump on it. Like a miniature camel."

"Nae, 'tis lovely, with the most kissable little nub at the end." He demonstrated with a swift press of his mouth to said nub.

"Yer ridiculous." Kendra laughed again. "Of all the things. *My nose.* 'Tis my *worst* feature. My eyes are my strongest asset."

"I disagree, but then I find everythin' about ye exceptional." He said this as his lips hovered a mere inch from hers. "Please seriously contemplate becomin' my countess, Kendra love. It will give me somethin' pleasant to ponder while I'm away from ye, and somethin' to look forward to when I return."

Like the draw of a magnet, her attention sank to his lips so very close to hers. She wanted his mouth on hers. Needed to taste him. More so than she required her next breath of air.

Did he deliberately torment her?

Was he demanding an answer before he satisfied her hunger?

What could it hurt to say she'd *think* about becoming the Countess of Montforth? She wasn't agreeing to do so. Broden hadn't even proposed. This thing blossoming between them was in the early stages, and it was much too soon to commit to something as serious as marriage.

But she could *consider* wedding him.

If only he'd kiss her again. And again. And again.

"Aye," she said, cupping his lightly stubbled jaw with one palm. "I'll think on it. *If* ye kiss me."

NINE

Sommerley Parke House
Near Carlisle, England
Five weeks later

Whisky glass in hand, temper high, and mood brooding, Broden gazed out the study's tall window, scowling at the snow-covered ground. The infernal white stuff had sifted from the skies for nearly a fortnight off and on. Good thing Liam had returned to Scotland three weeks ago at Broden's insistence.

He was a newlywed, after all.

Broden had bid Liam carry a message to Kendra. A vow he'd be bound for Scotland at the first opportunity.

The quartet of Scotsmen had made the trip to Sommerley Parke House in record time. And within three days of arrival at his primary estate, the foursome had set off for London.

That trip proved a colossal waste of time. Roxdale's horse had slipped on ice, tossing the duke onto his noble arse. He'd suffered a fractured wrist and wasn't of any help introducing Broden to society.

Just as well, since he'd little interest in hobnobbing with elitist snobs, which would further delay his homecoming. He might be an English earl now, but Scotland would always be his home.

Naturally, Roxdale's tumble was an unfortunate accident, but he'd eagerly returned to Trentwick Castle, his ducal family seat, and his new bride, the former Marjorie Kennedy. No one had anticipated a match between those two either.

Broden had called at the bank and, after verifying his identity and procuring the documents Oswald had provided him, had taken ownership of a sizable fortune.

A *very* sizable fortune.

No wonder Edwin *Archibald* had so enthusiastically anticipated inheriting.

Arching his back, Broden blew out a long breath before tossing back the rest of his whisky. His shoulder scarcely pained him at all, though now and again, if he moved suddenly, the almost-healed wound was wont to ache.

He'd discovered his illustrious relative mysteriously absent from London's social scene. Edwin hadn't been seen at his favorite haunts, or his lodgings either. He might've retired to the country for the winter, Broden supposed. Still, he'd like to make his kin's acquaintance to better judge the man's involvement in the plot to dispose of him.

Oswald hadn't mentioned precisely when Edwin had approached him about coming into the earldom. In truth, if Broden's cousin was responsible for the attempt on his life, he was likely shrewd enough to disappear for a time.

Oddly, Edwin wasn't the only person to up and vanish.

Oswald hadn't returned from his visit to Broden in Scotland.

Highly worrisome.

Oswald's business partner, Rufus Flowerplay, as short and

round as Oswald was tall and lean, was in quite a dither about his absence. He'd notified the authorities, but without any indication of foul play, there was aught they could do.

What had happened to Oswald after he departed the Toadstool Inn and Tavern?

Adding Broden's recuperation period, Oswald had been absent for almost two months. Broden couldn't help but suspect he might, indeed, have met with violence at the hands of the same fiend who'd tried to kill him. Everything, including motive, pointed to Edwin Archibald Wiggins McGregor.

Since Broden had left Eytone Hall, nothing suspicious had occurred to raise his concern. As far as attacks on his person, that was. Still, he wasn't mollified into laxity. Whoever wanted him dead was still out there biding his time.

Precisely where did Oswald fit in the puzzle?

That merited investigating.

Toward that end, Camden Kennedy had agreed to put his sleuthing skills to work, and even now, sought the whereabouts of Oswald and Edwin. A former smuggler and occasional covert agent, he was adept at slipping in and out of places without being seen. Camden also possessed an uncanny ability to procure information. Information others preferred remained hidden.

Only Bryston McPherson remained with Broden at Sommerley, much to Narcissa, Lady Montforth's discomfiture. Like an anxious mother hen, she rushed her enthralled daughters out of his presence whenever Bryston entered the room.

What did she think?

He was going to abduct the lasses and hold them for ransom?

Bryston only grinned and winked at the girls, which sent

them into fits of giggles and caused their mother to turn a starchy, blue-eyed gaze upon him. The two—*or was it thrice?*—occasions Broden had seen her in the company of her offspring.

True, Bryston's scarred face, long blond hair—the sides pulled back and secured in a messy knot—and tattoos on his arms and beringed fingers lent themselves to a rascally, swashbuckler's appearance. As did the ever-present sword and dirk at his waist. Broad of shoulder and easy of temperament, he took the countess's anxious scurrying about in stride.

What would she do if she knew Bryston McPherson had been a privateering buccaneer at one time, and Camden had smuggled his goods?

From his observations so far, Lady Montforth wasn't the fainting sort. Nonetheless, Broden was convinced her ladyship would find a way to rid the household of what she considered unsuitable riffraff.

He was similarly certain that he was lumped into that category as well, though she dared not voice her opinion to his face.

She was, after all, wholly dependent on his benevolence, as were her daughters.

He pitied her that.

A woman's lot wasn't easy.

Pulling his earlobe, he glowered at the pile of correspondences and other documents demanding his attention atop the oversized mahogany desk. Everything about Sommerley Parke House was grand and large.

He'd received so many bloody invitations that he could paper his entire house in Scotland with them. And he had not attended a single event thus far.

Much to Lady Montforth's consternation and frequent vocal objections. She was out of mourning and expected him to accompany her on her social jaunts. Her mistake for putting her confidence in him.

Broden was no fool. He well knew most of the invites were sent out of curiosity by those eager to meet the new, barbaric Scottish Earl of Montforth.

Eyebrows pulled together into an unforgiving line, he turned his mouth down.

He probably ought to hire a secretary or a man of business or both. But how did one go about such a thing? How did one find someone trustworthy and efficient?

Roxdale might know. Even Liam would, come to think of it.

He'd write and ask them both.

Lady Montforth had hinted, broadly and often, that she could recommend such a person. But given she also presumed Oswald to be a "Solicitor of superior character, impeccable decorum, and advanced acumen," Broden didn't put faith in her preferences.

In all likelihood, the countess secretly desired to influence him via his man of business. She'd soon learn he wasn't easily swayed or manipulated.

Sighing, he forced himself to sit in the comfortable leather desk chair and thumbed through the letters. He first searched for any from Eytone Hall. Mother had written last week and said, while she enjoyed the hospitality of the MacKays, that if Broden didn't return soon, she meant to go home.

Not to Glenawayshire, which she diligently sought to refurbish as he'd asked, but to their own cozy house. She maintained she wouldn't take up residence at Glenawayshire until he did as well.

That worried him no small amount, even if Liam's men continued to guard her.

Heaving a disgruntled sigh, he poured another dram of whisky.

Damn the delays. Damn the weather, which made travel nearly impossible right now. Damn his duties and responsibilities. Others had depended upon him before, but never in the quantities and degrees they did now.

Six females' every need and comfort rested upon him. Not to mention the extensive staff here and skeletal staff at four— *or was it five?*—more residences.

Swearing beneath his breath, he picked up another letter, examining the unfamiliar penmanship.

No' from Kendra either

She'd sent three short correspondences, to which he'd promptly responded. God only knew how long it had taken for their delivery. Given the inclement weather, no post could be transported in a timely fashion at present.

Neither of them said much of import in their missives, other than reporting on their daily happenings. Broden wasn't the sort to wax poetic or pen flowery phrases. He'd rather tell her how he felt in person.

And neither was she one to put her emotions on paper and risk someone else reading them. She was an immensely private person and held her feelings close to her chest. Yet she'd managed to wholly and entirely enchant him.

Just when they'd been on the cusp of something magnificent and magical developing between them, he'd had to leave. He might've postponed his departure, but eventually he would've needed to deal with those same matters.

Better sooner rather than later.

Once he'd settled things here, hired a reliable man of business, and replaced the ancient steward, whom he'd found sleeping every time he'd desired a word, he could trot along with his life.

His life with Kendra.

A pleasurable warmth spread from his gut outward that couldn't be attributed to the rather good whisky.

Nonetheless, lurking at the forefront of his mind hovered the knowledge that someone wanted him dead. Yes, it was better he remained at Sommerley, luring the killer away from Eytone Hall, Kendra, and his mother.

But did that put his wards and their mother in jeopardy?

Another question remained too.

How much time and effort should he allow before giving up the hunt for his assassin? What he should do was set a trap. That idea had real merit. Entice Edwin or his henchman into making a stupid move and revealing themselves.

But how?

Time to ponder that later, he supposed. But not too much later. He was deuced eager to be on his way. He'd believed he'd be back in Scotland by now, wooing Kendra, but had greatly underestimated how much was required of him once he'd claimed the earldom.

More fool he.

He'd always been a man who kept busy, but he grudgingly admitted there was more to this peerage business than he'd realized. At least, that was, if a noble took his responsibilities seriously. Broden never did anything in half-measures, and his role as the Earl of Montforth was no exception.

Managing the countess was no small accomplishment either. Narcissa was a deceptively serene woman, quiet and poised, quite lovely in truth. But with a stubborn streak wider than the Atlantic Ocean. And she had very decided opinions about what was expected of him when she deigned to speak to him at all.

Though only a year Broden's senior, she'd taken it upon herself to hint she could suggest young ladies she deemed qualified to be the next countess. Although she'd conceded, there was no *need* for him to rush into a marriage. He was young, after all.

Their first argument had occurred when he informed her that he'd already selected a lass to become his wife.

Never had he been so completely and politely taken to task. A Scotswoman not of noble birth was simply *not* appropriate, Narcissa staunchly maintained. Such a woman would never be accepted by Society, nor by Narcissa.

He might've suggested she mind her own business in less than gentlemanly terms.

If it hadn't been for his wards, he would've moved the countess to the dower house, but he'd inspected the place when he'd first arrived, and with only five bedchambers, two of which were for servants, he didn't have the heart to make her toddle off with her boisterous brood.

After meeting her sunny-haired daughters, Amaryllis, Bergenia, Celosia, Dianella, and Eustoma, ages nine, seven, four, three, and six months, each named after flora and in alphabetical order, he'd found himself surprisingly taken by the energetic but sweet-natured lasses.

Their haughty mother, not so much.

Her deceased sons, Standish Jr. and Harry, had been spared the horror of floral names.

A rap at the door interrupted his reflections, and he lifted his head. "Come."

TEN

Lady Montforth sailed into the room, her pink gown styled in the very latest fashion—according to her—billowed extra wide due to her panniers. She never quietly slipped into a chamber.

Each time, she made a grand entrance, clearly a woman accustomed to receiving a great deal of attention. At this moment, however, acute displeasure etched her regal features. Achieving a modicum of poise, she clasped her hands before her.

"Forgive the interruption, my lord, but several Scottish *persons* have arrived at the *front* entrance. Morris was prepared to send them on their way straightaway, but they insist upon seeing you at once." She elevated her perfect nose and sniffed disdainfully. "Rather loudly and forcefully, I might add."

"Where are they now?" Broden rose, stacking his unopened letters into a pile before putting the letter opener in the desk drawer.

Who the devil would've traveled here in this unfriendly weather?

Camden?

Possibly.

But who else?

Had he located Oswald? That would assuredly explain the unexpected call.

Broden's heartbeat quickened in anticipation.

Bryston slipped into the room, his features unreadable, but his posture suggesting he was battle-ready. One hand resting on his dirk, he took a position beside the door.

Broden spared him a hasty glance.

Precisely what was he guarding against?

The new arrivals?

"Ye dinna ken who they are, Narcissa?"

She shot him a look of sheer astonishment, very much as if he were a drooling imbecile. "As *I* didn't answer the door and am unacquainted with *any* Scots, save you and your four associates, how could I possibly know, my lord?"

She adamantly refused to address him by his given name. He assumed it wasn't as much out of deference as her dislike of all things Scottish.

"I shan't have my daughters upset by your ill-mannered acquaintances. I heard the shouting from my sitting room, and—"

The study door burst open with such force the panel slammed into the bookshelf behind the door with a startling thud.

Liam, Kendra, Graeme and Camden Kennedy, Logan Rutherford, and Coburn Wallace surged into the somber chamber. Disheveled, covered in travel grime, and the men all sporting beard stubble, they appeared exhausted.

And apprehensive.

A startled yelp sounding rather like a giant rodent escaped Narcissa, and she stumbled backward, holding a hand to her throat. Cutting Broden a panicked side-eyed glance, she swallowed convulsively.

"Why are these heathen Scots here? What do they want with us? Oh, Lord, they'll slay us all," she fairly squeaked, her face blanching. "Broden, you've already been shot by some blackguard. Have you no care for your wards' or my wellbeing?"

"They'll no' harm ye or the lasses," he growled, his patience spent.

As one, the new arrivals' gazes took in the countess. Equally of interest, as one, their countenances snapped closed, much like shutters secured before a pending storm.

What in God's holy name was Camden doing with them? And why had so many arrived at once? Their very numbers bespoke ominous news, perhaps even a threat of danger.

To whom?

His wards?

Kendra?

At once, Broden was tense and alert. "What's happened?"

Kendra rushed forward, snowflakes still covering her cloak, her boots leaving wet tracks on the plush carpet. She pushed her hood down, exposing reddened cheeks and wide, worried dove-gray eyes.

She was breathtaking, and he feasted his ravenous gaze upon her, longing to ensnare her in his embrace and plunder her sweet mouth. His focus dropped to those tantalizing lips, and the tiniest smile twitched at the corners.

Ah, she knew *exactly* what he was thinking.

"We need to speak with ye." She turned a gimlet eye on Narcissa. "Alone."

He'd never seen Kendra behave in this manner. So coldly and rudely to someone she'd not been introduced to. Well, *he'd* been on the receiving end of her sharp tongue and blistering glares, but they had a history together.

She was in a high fettle, and none of his friends denied her assertion.

Something was drastically wrong.

Narcissa drew herself up, giving Kendra a scathing assessment from head to toe, undoubtedly finding her wanting from her haughty, pinched expression.

"What is the meaning of this intrusion?" Apparently, she'd decided the newcomers weren't going to slit her throat or raze the house. "How dare you traipse into *my* home with your muddy boots dripping snow all over *my* floors and rudely dismiss me?" She turned her wrathful gaze upon Broden. "Broden, are you going to permit this inexcusable insult by this *riffraff*?"

Kendra didn't back down. If anything, she set her delicate jaw firmer, steely resolve in her unrelenting gaze. "Lady Montforth, I presume?" she queried, her tone as frosty as the outdoors as she removed her gloves.

Narcissa condescended to lower her chin a fraction in acknowledgment, though her nostrils flared as if she smelled fresh manure or offal.

Until now, she'd kept this side of her personality subdued.

Broden's already low opinion of her plummeted further.

He'd believed her vain, pampered, and cosseted, a woman accustomed to having her way, and one who appreciated and lauded her elevated status. But this haughty termagant had the audacity to look down her nose at the women he loved.

Narcissa had best have a care.

Insult Kendra, and there *would* be consequences.

Eyebrow raised, Kendra, in turn, took Lady Montforth's measure.

Though her expression remained impassive, contempt darkened her eyes to the color of the sky before a tempest. "We've ridden for two days straight in that hellish weather outside bringin' news of utmost import to Broden. News that is confidential and urgent. So ye'll excuse us for no' mincin' words or wastin' time with niceties."

One of the men concealed a bark of laughter with a strangled cough. Likely Wallace.

"*You* dare address Lord Montforth by his given name?" Narcissa demanded, all outraged self-righteousness. "Your impertinence is beyond galling. Know your place, impudent chit."

"As I've kent Broden since I was a wee lass, I'll continue to address him as such." Kendra didn't flinch under the countess's snide disapproval. "Now, if ye'll excuse us? We've urgent matters to discuss."

Narcissa turned a frigid eye upon the new arrivals before defiantly jutting her pointed chin upward. "I'm not leaving unless Lord Montforth directs me to."

Kendra's eyebrows shied higher, and her mouth went tight when Narcissa sidled closer to Broden and placed her hand on his forearm, almost possessively.

What was this?

She'd never touched him before.

In fact, she avoided him whenever possible.

Directing a pointed look at Narcissa's hand, Kendra brought what Broden knew to be a carefully bland gaze to his. Her eyes fairly shouted for him to explain.

His eyebrows practically touching, his attention shifted between the women.

"Narcissa, please ask Morris to see to refreshments for everyone. And plenty of them." If they'd ridden as hard as Kendra vowed they had, they were undoubtedly famished. "Hot tea for Miss MacKay, and somethin' more substantial for the gentlemen."

Jaw slack, Narcissa blinked several times before she

snapped her mouth closed with an audible click and narrowed her eyes to furious slits. "Are you dismissing me in my own home when I outrank these..." She fluttered her hand contemptuously at Kendra and the men as she searched for an appropriate word. "*People*?"

She made the word sound like a curse.

He'd dare that and much more, by God. How dare *she* insult his friends? His almost betrothed? Treat them like they were excrement on her dainty, very expensive buckled shoe?

"Firstly..." Ire made his tone razor-sharp. "Ye have nae idea who they are. So ye havena any way of kentin' if ye outrank them. Secondly, I dinna give a rats hairy arse about rank."

"You..." She gasped, going pale and weakly clasping a hand to her bosom. "You are so uncouth as to swear in a lady's presence?"

Now she became a wilting rose?

The Scotsmen, lined up inside the doorway like watchful sentinels, remained stonily silent, their flint-like gazes pinned on the rather wan-faced Lady Montforth.

Never one for female histrionics or dramatics, Kendra rolled her eyes as she unfastened her cloak. He had no doubt it took every bit of her considerable restraint not to tell Narcissa precisely what she thought of her. Which, he had no doubt, would assure a dramatic fit of the vapors.

"And I'll remind ye, Lady Montforth—kindly because yer station is as new to ye as mine is to me—*I* am the lord here," he said. "My word is law, no' yers. These are *my* friends, and ye will treat them with the same respect and regard ye would any of yer pompous and illustrious acquaintances. Is that understood?"

For several moments, he believed she might refuse. A battle raged full-on in her defiant gaze. Finally, lips pursed tight as a goose's back end, she gave a stiff nod. "Am I to understand you expect me to entertain—*her?*"

Struggling to wrestle her scorn under control, she turned her pale blue eyes on Kendra.

"Miss Kendra MacKay," Broden said. "Sister to Liam MacKay, Baron Penderhaven." He motioned to Liam. "Beside him is Laird Graeme Kennedy and his brother Camden Kennedy."

They nodded, stern and unenthusiastic greetings.

"Those two gentlemen"—he indicated Logan and Coburn—"are Laird Logan Rutherford and his cousin, Coburn Wallace."

Though not of the English peerage, each of the Scots held elevated positions by virtue of their births as well. Not that he expected Narcissa to be aware or revere them as was their due.

"Nae, ye needna entertain me, my lady," Kendra said, draping her cloak over a nearby chair. She wore a simple burgundy riding habit, the color a perfect complement to her tousled rich, molasses-colored hair and wind-ripened lips.

Narcissa's eyes narrowed again, and she cinched her mouth impossibly tighter into a terse, disapproving line.

"She's not *at all* suitable, my lord." She shook her intricately coiffed, white-blonde head, something akin to malice creeping into her refined voice. "No, no, I say, she'll never do. Most unfitting."

Broden's fury swelled and crested like violent, surging waves blown ashore during a hurricane. "Enough," he warned in a low, I've-had-enough-of-your-shite tone.

"What *can* you be thinking?" Narcissa prattled on, either unaware of the storm brewing or uncaring. "You have a position to uphold. There are certain expectations of a peer. Strictures and protocols that *must* be observed. Surely,

Broden, you must understand how very unsuitable such a creature is."

Creature? By God and all the saints, he'd banish her to a cottage in Barra in the Outer Hebrides.

She flicked a contemptuous glance at Kendra.

Shoulders squared, her head raised in defiance, she unflinchingly met Narcissa's spiteful glare. A beautiful warrior ready to take on her foe.

Pride nudged aside a portion of Broden's wrath—a very small portion.

"For heaven's sake," Narcissa blathered on as if she believed any of them cared a whit about her odious, biased opinions. "She admitted to traveling with four men without the benefit of a female companion. Some would suggest..."

Harsh inhalations and Broden's low, threatening growl met the insinuation. He swung a quelling look at her as the others stiffened in affront at her vulgar innuendo.

"Make her your mistress, if you must, my lord. But most assuredly, *she* cannot become your countess." She finished, smug and confident she'd succeeded in squashing Kendra beneath her expensive silk shoe.

"My lady," Liam started, fire in his eyes, but Kendra held up her hand.

"*She* is standin' right here and can hear every insultin' word ye are spoutin'." She folded her arms and took the countess's measure again, this time slowly, deliberately, and contemptuously. "It seems to me there's a lot more to bein' a lady of quality and refinement than who one's father and mother might've been."

Narcissa stepped forward, her hands half-curled into fists. "He'll never marry *you*," she spat, stomping her foot. Actually, stomping in the same petulant manner three-year-old Dianella had yesterday when denied a fourth biscuit. "I shall not permit it. A Scottish strumpet the next Countess of Montforth? Never!"

ELEVEN

"What the hell is she blatherin' about?" That came from Graeme Kennedy.

Camden whistled, and Logan and Wallace traded bewildered looks.

Liam strode forward and put a protective arm around Kendra's shoulders. "Consider yer words carefully, madam. I'll no' stand by and allow ye to insult my sister."

Kendra sent him a grateful smile.

How she itched to slap the arrogant harpy's face. She'd all but implied Kendra was a whore. She refused to give Lady Montforth the satisfaction of seeing how much the cruel woman's cutting words had wounded and humiliated her.

She wasn't surprised by her ladyship's venom, given what Camden had learned about Lady Narcissa. Her pretty outward trappings concealed an evil heart and a blacker soul. She was the devil's handmaiden if there ever was one.

Her poor daughters.

What would become of the unfortunate dears with a mother like that? It was profound good fortune that Broden was now their legal guardian.

"My choice of a countess, my lady," Broden gritted out through clenched teeth, "is absolutely none of yer business, and ye'll have nae say in the matter. Ye would be wise to retire to yer chamber and remain there until I summon ye."

Kendra wanted to launch herself into his arms. Not only because he defended her so vehemently, but because she'd missed him dreadfully. And now that he stood but a few feet away, she longed to kiss him. To tell him how much she realized she loved him while he was gone.

For she did love him. Absolutely and profoundly. Unconditionally and irrevocably.

Now that she had admitted it to herself, it had become glaringly obvious that she had for some time. How she'd missed the signs, she couldn't venture to guess. But her focus had ever been on Broden's flaws and not his numerous exemplary qualities.

She couldn't prevent the small—fine, perhaps not so very small—satisfied smile she directed toward the countess.

Broden strode to the bell pull and gave the dark green and gold braided silk cord a firm tug. Not more than three seconds after Broden summoned him, the butler entered. Probably lurking in the corridor eavesdropping as any butler worth his salt was wont to do.

"Yes, my lord?" He didn't so much as slide a furtive glance toward the brawny Scots or his highly agitated mistress.

"My friends are hungry and thirsty after their long journey," Broden said. "Please ask Cook to prepare refreshments for them, as well as tea for Miss MacKay and ale for the men."

"I took it upon myself to ask Mrs. Wilson to assemble a hardy repast upon their arrival, sir." Morris angled his head. "I believe it is nearly prepared."

"How dare you, Morris? You overstep your authority. Do you not value your position at all?" The countess all but hissed, "I should dismiss you without a reference right this moment. I am still the mistress here, am I not?"

Not for much longer, Kendra would wager.

Despite Lady Montforth's tirade, Morris's countenance remained impassive, and he never missed a blink. "The food will be ready shortly, my lord. Shall I also have chambers prepared for our honored guests?"

Morris still hadn't made eye contact with the seething woman. One might gather he didn't hold her in high esteem, nor did he feel obligated to cede to her wishes. That he directed his requests to Broden said much about his opinion of the countess.

Kendra liked the man.

He was a good judge of character.

"No, of course, you shall not. Of all the absurd suggestions. They won't be staying, you insolent, presumptuous beef wit." Lady Montforth all but frothed in her agitation. "I cannot have such uncouth company beneath the same roof as my darlings."

Her darlings she only ventured to see once a fortnight?

"Ye may go, Morris." Broden offered an apologetic smile. "And thank ye for yer thoughtfulness. Please do have the chambers prepared."

An agitated, most unladylike noise very near a growl echoed from the Lady Montforth's direction.

With a half bow and the veriest raising of his noble brow toward the sulking countess, the butler departed the study.

No sooner had the door closed behind him than Broden turned on her.

"Once again, I'll remind ye, Narcissa, that I pay the wages of every staff member in this household. Morris is accountable to me, and ye owe him an apology for yer uncalled-for rudeness. However, it will have to wait, as I've exhausted my reserve of patience where ye are concerned. Ye've also exhausted yer welcome in this household."

Lady Montforth's bravado slipped a notch, and she licked her lower lip. "Perhaps I was a bit overly—"

"Madam. Leave. Now." Broden's clipped tone countenanced no argument.

If her ladyship knew Broden at all, she'd understand he was at the end of his tether and barely keeping his fury under control.

With a lofty tilt of her chin, she swept to the door and pulled her skirts aside as if the Scots might soil her gown if her hem brushed their legs.

Liam angled his head toward Logan. "Follow her and make sure she disna leave her chamber. Also, check every single item that goes in and out of her chamber, and nae one, no' even her daughters, are to enter her rooms."

"Aye." Logan gave a terse nod before departing the study.

"The rest of ye monitor the entrances," Liam ordered. "Camden, ye can fill Bryston in on the way."

They, too, left at once.

"What was that all about?" Broden asked. "I'll warrant Lady Montforth was discourteous beyond measure, but ye needna treat her like a prisoner. And why do the entrances need watchin'? I assure ye, there are far more than four ways in and out of this house."

"We've more men outside guardin' the perimeter." Liam traveled to the window and unceremoniously shoved the curtain aside.

Kendra touched Broden's arm. "Broden, we have reason to believe she's behind yer assassination attempt. That's why we came here straightaway."

He scowled and crossed his arms, resting his lean hips against the edge of the desk. "I presume ye've learned somethin', and I'll hear it soon enough." His attention shifted to Kendra. "But why are ye here, Kendra? If there's a threat, ye should've remained at Eytone Hall. 'Tis safer there."

A hint of the old, defiant Kendra flared to life. She tamped down her temper. Worry and concern were behind his clipped words. Instead, she arched her eyebrows in a challenge. "Ye ken me better than that."

Liam snorted and shook his head. "Ye try tellin' my sister that drivel. I did, and she wasna havin' any of it." Affection and frustration gleamed in the look he bathed her with. "Ye ken, as well as I, how stubborn she can be. She threatened to journey here by herself. On horseback."

Broden closed his eyes for a long blink as if greatly pained.

Or annoyed. Or frustrated. Worried. Confused…

"At least if she traveled with us, I could keep her safe," Liam said, peering out the beveled panes.

Kendra brushed a lock of hair off her forehead as she met Broden's irate stare. "I would've done it too, because I would've gone mad waitin' for word." Despite her brother's presence, she took his hand. "Ye would've done the same thing if I were in danger, Broden, and dinna deny it. We are alike in that."

Sighing and his chest deflating with the exhalation, he gathered her into his powerful arms. "Aye, I would have done."

She went willingly, relishing the protective band of his arms encircling her.

Liam cleared his throat, a hint of mirth creasing the corners of his eyes. "I presume after Lady Montforth's ragin' and this touchin' show of affection." He gestured between Kendra and Broden. "This means ye intend to ask for Kendra's hand in marriage?"

Surely Broden wouldn't embrace her in Liam's presence if

that weren't his intent. She tilted her head up, admiring his strong jaw, and sought his umber-brown gaze.

Hunger and passion and love shone there.

Love for her.

When she thought how close she'd come to missing out on loving this man and being loved by him, she could weep.

"Aye." He brushed her cheek tenderly with his knuckle. "I'd make her my countess this verra minute if she was willin'."

"She's willin'," Kendra said rather breathlessly.

Too blasted bad, her brother stood but a few feet away, or she'd show Broden precisely how willing she was.

Liam chuckled as he left his inspection of the outdoors and wandered to the center of the room. "I always wondered if the constant sparks between the two of ye were anythin' more than animosity. I'm glad 'twas, since it pained me to have two of the people I most cared about constantly sparin'. I'm well-pleased to be able to soon call ye brother."

He clasped Broden's hand in a hearty handshake.

"What's this about Narcissa possibly being behind my shootin'?" Broden features went granite hard as he absently touched his shoulder. "Now that I think on it, she did mention I'd been shot. I didna tell her that."

She knew because she'd hired the killer.

At least all signs pointed in that direction.

Kendra heaved an unsteady sigh. "Camden trailed Edwin McGregor to Scotland. McGregor was tryin' to find ye. Someone also made an attempt on his life. He, however, saw and recognized his assailant."

Broden went perfectly still, a warrior's practiced scowl darkening his features. "Och? Who?"

"Oswald," Liam and Kendra said simultaneously.

Kendra continued. "Naturally, as I'd never met Oswald, I didna realize he was the man who'd shot ye. However, after a discussion with Mr. McGregor, it became very clear to me that Oswald was your shooter too. The description of the man matched Oswald's perfectly."

Broden swiped a hand through his soft hair, lines of tension creasing the granite planes of his face. She so wanted to kiss away his concern and agitation. Make him forget, just for a time, that someone wanted him dead.

"Oswald? But why? It disna make sense." Three deep grooves puckering his forehead, he paced to the window and then back. "How do ye ken Edwin McGregor is tellin' the truth?"

"The man was scared spitless. He remained in hidin' for a month afterward, and then it occurred to him that if Oswald had tried to kill him, mightn't he also try to eliminate ye?" Liam exchanged a guarded glance with Kendra. "He darkened his hair and traveled under an assumed name while pretendin' to be a reverend. He's no' exactly the courageous sort. He claims he sought ye out hopin' ye could catch Oswald."

"Where is he now?" Concern shadowed Broden's face, even as a calculating gleam shone in his eyes.

"He's bein' held at Kennedy's keep. Until we could verify his tale, it seemed wisest no' to let him blunder about." An ironic smile quirked Kendra's mouth. "I still had my doubts about him until he eagerly agreed to the confinement. He's good and truly terrified."

Broden paced back across the study's plush Turkish carpet, his hands clasped behind his back. "It disna make sense. How does Oswald benefit from mine or Edwin's deaths?"

Liam, now resting a shoulder against the fireplace mantel, raised his gaze from studying the flames.

Kendra touched her chin thoughtfully. "Mayhap the question isna how does Oswald benefit or who benefits the most if the heirs are dead, but who has the most to lose if they're alive?"

Broden halted and brought his attention overhead to the ornate plasterwork ceiling. "Narcissa?"

"Aye." Kendra firmed her mouth. "We think Oswald is nearby, and we think he's workin' in conjunction with the countess." She cut Liam a swift look, days of worry catching up to her and sending dread throttling through her every pore. "In truth, Camden is the one who speculates that's the situation. 'Tis a bit disconcertin' just how calculatin' his mind is."

Broden tugged his earlobe. "I think a candid discussion with the countess is in order straightaway. With witnesses. That woman can tie knots in a man with her fishwife's tongue."

Kendra would rather not endure the horrid woman's presence for a minute more, but Broden was correct.

A knock sounded at the door.

"Enter," Broden bade.

Morris entered pushing a tea cart. His stoic gaze circled the room, a question in his eyes. "Your refreshments as requested, my lord."

He silently asked where the others were.

Kendra's stomach growled, and she placed her hand over her hollow tummy. None of them had eaten since yesterday afternoon, except for oatcakes while they rode. Bone weary, she wanted nothing more than to take a hot bath and climb between clean sheets.

Preferably with Broden.

She indulged in a wicked half-smile.

He'd awoken desire in her, and she was eager to have her passion stoked into a wildfire.

However, such comforts and fantasies would have to wait.

Uncovering the countess's involvement was paramount to

Broden's safety. Perhaps she knew where Oswald was at this moment too. He might've even followed them to Sommerley Parke House, and he was undoubtedly desperate to cover his tracks after two failed murder attempts.

Served the countess right for hiring a novice for such a gruesome task.

"I've asked my friends to act as sentries, Morris." Broden gestured to Kendra to help herself to the tea cart's contents.

Ah, so he had heard her stomach's relentless complaining.

"We've reason to believe an assassin is nearby," he said.

The butler's jaw slackened, and his eyes rounded for only a second before he composed his features. "May I ask if the children are in any danger?"

Broden had liked the stuffy chap from the onset, but that his first concern was for the lasses raised him higher in his estimation.

"We dinna believe so, but it wouldna hurt to assign yer most trusted footmen to guard the nursery. Men who are loyal to me." An unspoken message passed between him and the majordomo.

"Just so, my lord." A flicker of understanding sparked in Morris's eyes and he dipped his head. "You are aware of the secret passageways in the house?"

"Aye, though I've no' toured them myself as yet."

Secret passageways?

Not unusual in larger mansions or castles. Throughout history, people had used those sorts of passages for everything from clandestine assignations to smuggling or spying.

Kendra inspected the study more thoroughly. Were there any in here?

"One leads directly from her ladyship's bedchamber to a hidden panel in the library," Morris offered.

Broden jerked his full attention to the prim servant. "The library? Next door?"

"Indeed, my lord." Did Morris's lips twitch the merest bit? Was that a glow of triumph in his placid gaze?

He'd seen to it her ladyship met with her comeuppance.

Another reason to treat servants with respect and dignity. They knew absolutely everything that went on in a household, and far better for them to be one's allies than foes. Something the countess would've done well to practice.

Broden tore to the study door, calling beneath his breath, "Follow me. Morris, have my men at the ready outside the library's exits."

"Yes, my lord." The staid fellow practically flew down the passageway. This was probably the most exciting misadventure he'd ever participated in.

Definitely, no love lost between him and the countess. The truth was, from what Kendra had witnessed of the woman, she'd behaved like an abusive virago.

"There are three doorways into the library, plus the hidden passage," Broden said as they rushed along. "One leads to this corridor. Another provides an escape onto a terrace paralleling the lawns and gardens. And another very small door is situated on the far side of the upper gallery. I presumed it led to an attic or storage area of some sort."

What if they were too late?

Had the countess flown already?

Once outside the library, Broden lifted a large finger to his lips. "If she's already inside or in the passage, we dinna want to alert her."

Kendra's heart beat wildly in her breast.

Perhaps the countess would attempt to send a message to Oswald. Surely if she were working in conjunction with him, she knew his whereabouts. *The despicable weasel.*

Broden cautiously depressed the handle and the well-maintained door slid open without a sound. He turned sideways and leaned to peer into the room. Lifting his hand, he motioned them forward.

"'Tis empty," he whispered.

Not more than fifteen minutes had passed since Lady Montforth had stormed from the study. Nonetheless, Kendra worried her lower lip, afraid they'd missed her. Well, even if she had sneaked out to send a message, she'd have to come back.

No mother would leave her children behind.

They filed through the doorway, and she couldn't help but be enthralled at the gorgeous room.

Beautifully carved shelves held thousands of books. Three burgundy brocade divans arranged in a U-shape sat before a black and white marble fireplace. Several comfortable armchairs were placed about the room in groups of two or four with sturdy tables nearby.

Most impressive, though, was an intricate spiral staircase ascending to an upper gallery that she immediately wanted to explore.

All of this—the house and furnishings and grand library —was Broden's. All of this majesty and wealth. Yet the man she knew didn't care about affluent displays.

A fire burned in the hearth, but no candles lit the room. Shadows obscured the farthest corners of the chamber, and only a thin ribbon of grayish light shone through the open draperies. Without a doubt, more snow portended.

Advancing farther into the chamber, she silently lamented she hadn't thought to snatch a scone off the tea cart to take the edge off her hunger.

"Where's the secret passage?" Liam asked softly.

Broden indicated a panel to the right of the fireplace. "There," he said in a hushed voice. "I kent about the passageway but wasna aware it connected to Narcissa's chamber."

He strode to the windows and peered out. Giving a satisfied nod, he faced them again and whispered, "Coburn and Graeme are outside."

He motioned to Kendra.

"Come, wait with me here." He took up a position near a window to the side of the velvet panels. "We can use the draperies as cover. Liam, ye hide over there."

He indicated the shelf to the fireplace's left.

Liam silently crossed to the other side, his tobacco-brown coat blending into the bookcase's dark walnut wood and the afternoon shadows. A slanted platform for perusing maps and other large documents was positioned atop a table at a diagonal angle, further obscuring his presence.

Broden took Kendra's hand, giving it a slight squeeze as he whispered in her ear. "Dinna do anythin' foolish. Let yer brother and me handle this. Narcissa may become violent. I only want ye here as a female witness."

His warm breath tickled her ear and sent scintillating currents of hot desire pulsing through her.

Rising to her toes, she spoke into his ear. "I missed ye."

Even in the gloomy half-light, she could see the desire glinting in his eyes. As always, his manly scent—soap, shaving lather, and a hint of spice—made her long to bury her face in his corded neck.

Several interminable moments passed, and just when Kendra was certain the countess had escaped them, a rasping creak echoed deep within the wall.

Stiffening, and on pins and needles, she held her breath.

Broden went rigid beside her and placed his palm on her shoulder in a silent warning. His touch took the edge off her nerves. But only the edge. God only knew what the countess was capable of.

The panel swung open with a rusty groan, and Lady Montforth crept out wearing a plain, drab brown cloak. Likely a servant's.

She took but three halting steps before Broden spoke.

"Goin' somewhere?"

Lady Montforth swung to face them, sheer loathing contorting her face. Her lips curled into a gloating sneer as she clumsily raised a blunderbuss from the folds of her cloak.

Oh, God.

TWELVE

Broden shoved Kendra behind him, blocking her from the pistol's aim. He cursed himself for a fool for not having anticipated Narcissa would be armed. For underestimating her deviousness and her determination.

The countess laughed, a tinny sound, bordering on unhinged.

Nae, no' borderin'. Chin deep in madness.

"How very touching. You're trying to protect your Scottish harlot." She shook her head, almost consolatory, as if explaining a complicated rule to an errant child. "You cannot be permitted to wed her, of course. Or anyone, for that matter. It just won't do." She blinked up at him benignly, completely in the grips of her insanity. "It would disrupt years and years of meticulous planning, you see."

Kendra poked her head around Broden's shoulder. "Why do ye care who he weds? Ye and yer daughters will be well-cared for and have everythin' ye could possibly require. He's a kind, generous man."

"Kendra, stay behind me," he practically growled when she edged even closer to his side. He'd seen tetched in the head

137

people before. One minute, they appeared perfectly sane and coherent, and the next, they frothed at the mouth, absolutely out of control.

What did she think to accomplish by defending him to this crazed woman, anyway?

On silent feet, Liam had skirted the display table and was now within a couple of yards of the countess. He but awaited Broden's signal to seize her from behind. Nonetheless, the manner in which she wielded the pistol called for caution.

"Children," Narcissa muttered, in bored tones. "Specifically, *male* offspring. He might sire a son." A befuddled frown pulled her eyebrows together. "Though, I suppose, there's no guarantee a male would live to adulthood." In a blink, her mien transformed into maniacal cunning. "I made certain mine didn't."

Shite. She *was* bloody insane.

Kendra choked on a strangled gasp and clutched Broden's arm, her nails digging into the flesh through his coat and shirt. "Ye...? Ye harmed yer own wee bairns?" Repugnance and incredulity thickened her voice, making it raspy.

God above. He swallowed against the acrid bile climbing his throat.

Narcissa gave a disinterested shrug as if she hadn't revealed a horrendous fact as casually as selecting which bonnet to wear to the park. "Philibius and I have been systematically disposing of Montforth heirs for years."

Did the dunderheaded woman think she could confess her crimes before witnesses and not pay the consequences? After all, there were three of them—although she wasn't aware of Liam's presence—and she only had one shot. Surely, she wasn't so addled that she didn't comprehend the truth of the situation.

Or mayhap, she was.

Vigilant, every sense on high alert and every muscle poised, ready to spring, Broden watched her as he would a viper about to strike. Mindful to keep his focus on her, lest she become aware of Liam stealthily stealing up behind her, he asked, "Why? Ye canna inherit and neither can yer daughters."

Releasing an exaggerated sigh, she worked her supercilious gaze over him.

"Fool. You are thinking like a typical man. I, however, possess a woman's shrewdness. A woman's dauntlessness, and I have had my fill of men governing my life. At my direction, and with a bit of incentive, Philibius made a few subtle *amendments* to the prior earl's will."

Broden could guess what those incentives were.

"Naturally, I cannot inherit any of the entailed properties," she said offhandedly as she slid a side-eyed look to the terrace.

The snow-blanketed grounds appeared serene and peaceful.

More than a dozen warriors lurked without, ready to vault into action at the snap of a finger. He hadn't a single misgiving Graeme and Coburn had their guns' sights trained on her, but if they were too far away, their shots mightn't hit their mark as intended.

He must keep her distracted. Prevent her from realizing the peril she was now in. Irrational people often reacted with a paranatural strength when cornered. "So why are ye disposin' of the Montforth heirs?"

Though he didn't dare glance in her direction, he heard Kendra's short breaths, felt the abhorrence for the countess radiating off her.

"*Silly.*" Narcissa giggled airily. "If no males remain in the line, I can—*will*—inherit everything else. It amounts to a substantial fortune and includes several properties and businesses. Have you any idea what that kind of freedom means to a woman like me? One who's been bred to be married off like a prize horse to the highest bidder? Whose only value is producing *sons*?"

"My God," Kendra breathed into his shoulder, her breasts pressed against him. "Ye truly are the devil's handmaiden. Why would Mr. Oswald agree to somethin' so vile?"

Sex. Money. Power. Control.

Mostly control.

Lady Montforth laughed as if Kendra had just shared an amusing jest. "You've seen the man. He's homely, stupid, and almost panting for female attention. But he's even hungrier for money. When he eliminates the last heir, I've promised him a hundred thousand pounds."

An envious cull like Oswald, a man who always coveted what others had and could never hope to have for himself, wouldn't be hard to sway to dastardliness.

A pretty pout formed on Narcissa's full, rosy mouth.

Perhaps even a forbidden kiss. A suggestive skimming of her hands. Seductive whispers in Oswald's ears of all he was missing and all she could give him--would *do* to him.

All lies, of course, designed to manipulate the weak-willed solicitor to do her foul bidding.

Unfortunately, a morally bankrupt sod like Oswald would leap at the chance to better his station. To claim a woman like Narcissa as his own.

Much like the black widow spider, she probably intended to dispose of Oswald too.

A crafty smile bent her mouth, her pale blue eyes peculiarly blank and fiendish at the same time. "That's a promise of a new life to a man like Oswald. An existence he could only fantasize about. He'll do *anything* to achieve that goal."

"Did ye honestly think ye could succeed with yer ludicrous

plan?" Broden was careful not to say demented or unhinged. Those drowning in lunacy couldn't face their derangement.

He shifted his stance, prepared to lunge and wrest the flintlock from her grasp.

"You will both precede me from the house." Shrewdness filtered into her features as she waived the weapon back and forth between him and Kendra. "If either of you attempts to alert the men I have no doubt are skulking about outside…" She cocked the hammer. "I shall shoot the other."

"Yer plan is doomed to fail." Kendra slipped out from behind Broden. Like a warrior princess, she faced Narcissa, brave and bold and beautiful. "Oswald didna kill Edwin McGregor, and when he followed Edwin to Scotland, he was captured."

Liam caught Broden's eye, a question in his.

With the merest flexing of his eyelids, he warned Liam to wait.

Furious at Kendra for endangering herself, he stifled his first reaction to shove her unceremoniously behind him once more. However, she'd obviously caught Narcissa off guard with her brilliant lie.

And that could be used to their advantage.

He'd scold her soundly afterward. Right now, he must concentrate on preventing Narcissa from shooting her.

Momentarily stunned at the unforeseen news, Narcissa blinked wildly. She tossed her head back, jutted her chin up, and surged forward, threatening Kendra with the gun. "You're lying, slut. I had a letter from Philibius two days ago telling me to meet him at the Tates' charred cottage today."

Good. Now Broden knew where Oswald was, *the bugger.*

Only the merest shifting of Liam's eyebrows acknowledged he'd made a mental note of the useful information.

Kendra shook her head, more hair tumbling from her pins.

"He's no' there. We coerced him into writin' that letter. He's been promised a reduced sentence if he identifies the mastermind behind the scheme. Otherwise, he'd hang for certain."

Where had she learned to lie like that?

A seasoned prostitute and swindler couldn't have fabricated such codswallop out of thin air with as much ease or expediency.

Oswald would hang, in any event, for attempted murder.

However, a woman of Narcissa's breeding and background probably knew little about penal codes or criminal sentences. Had little understanding she'd meet the same fate, no matter whether she cooperated or not.

She'd admitted to killing her sons. There'd be no redemption or mercy.

Christ. Broden was guardian to five lasses whose mother would hang for killing their brothers and father.

The girls must never know. *Never.*

He'd concoct a believable tale, and as tragic as it was that the lasses would grow up without their mother, he'd protect them from the sickening truth.

He must, for their sake.

"No, Philibius adores me. He wouldn't betray me." Confusion etched shadows across Narcissa's pallid features. Uncertainty battled with fury and insanity for dominance.

Shoving a glossy strand of hair behind her shoulder, Kendra gave a mocking laugh. "He was only too willin' to name ye. He laid everthin' at yer feet. Said ye planned every last detail. Vowed ye threatened to claim he imposed himself upon ye if he didna cooperate."

"Kendra," he warned, touching her wrist.

She might push the countess too far.

Narcissa gasped and, jerking as if backhanded, staggered

backward a pace. Her face twisting with umbrage, she aimed the barrel directly at Kendra's chest.

"That's a lie," she spat, her gaze shifting back and forth wildly. "'Twas all his idea. I knew he had a fondness for me. I could see it in his lovesick stares and pitiful sighs whenever he called upon Standish. And when he found me in tears one day after another beating by Standish, he pledged his love. Vowed to help me."

And now they had a full confession as well. Hopefully, men waited in the corridor, taking in every word.

Any sympathy Broden might've summoned for her abuse at the fourth earl's hands was soundly extinguished by her confession of slaying her sons.

"Ye do realize ye've confessed to multiple murders and plottin' to commit others in front of witnesses, dinna ye?" Broden deliberately drew her fury away from Kendra.

With the slightest incantation of his head, he gave Liam the signal.

As Narcissa swung his way, murderous wrath contorting her features and hatred in her eyes, he dove for Kendra. He shoved her to the floor and covered her body with his own.

Liam lunged for Narcissa at the same moment, wrapping his arms around her from behind and firmly striking her wrist, forcing her to drop the pistol.

The gun discharged with a deafening boom as it landed upon the floor.

She screamed and struggled, thrashing and violently striking out with her feet.

Jaw locked and features strained, Liam kept her contained, grunting and swearing beneath his breath.

At once, the terrace doors flew open, and Coburn and Graeme pounded into the chamber.

"Is everyone all right?" Graeme asked, rushing to kneel beside Broden and Kendra.

"Aye. I was but protectin' my future wife." Broden rolled off her, and, after rising, helped her stand.

Face pale as paper, but remarkably composed, Kendra gave him a shaky smile and leaned into his side, rubbing her right elbow. "That was—unexpected."

"But necessary." He pressed a kiss to her forehead. "Are ye all right?"

She nodded, eyeing the countess.

"Let me go!" Narcissa shrieked, kicking and bucking against Liam. "Unhand me. I am Lady Montforth, you filthy Scot. I'll see you hanged for this, you bastard."

"Can one of ye assist me?" he managed between grunts and curses. "Tie the countess's hands and find somethin' to gag her with."

Graeme made quick work of cutting the cords holding the draperies back and secured her hands behind her back as Coburn stuffed his neckcloth into her mouth with all of the care of stopping a leak in a skiff.

"Never heard a more foul-mouthed lady in my life," he said with satisfaction as the cloth muffled her shrieks and profanities.

Broden kissed the crown of Kendra's head again. "Lass, ye were spectacular, but if ye ever do anythin' so foolhardy again, I'll take my hand to yer backside."

He hugged her fiercely, and she cuddled against him like a cold kitten, seeking his warmth and comfort.

"Oswald's waitin' for Lady Montforth at a burned cottage owned by someone named Tate. Ask Morris if he kens where it is and prepare half a dozen men to go with us. Someone also needs to go for the magistrate." Broden tightened his embrace around Kendra.

"I'm fine," she murmured quietly, as if she understood his unspoken fear. "Really, I am. Just a trifle bruised."

"I'll ask the butler to send a footman for the magistrate," Coburn said, already striding toward the door. "I'll have the horses prepared too."

This situation could've gone much differently. Sweat born of stark terror for Kendra soaked Broden. A glint in Narcissa's eyes an instant before he tackled Kendra warned him: she meant to kill the woman he loved.

"Secure Lady Montforth somewhere where her daughters will no' come upon her," Broden said. "Preferably a room with nae windows. She's to have three guards present outside at all times. See that she has somethin' to eat and a cot."

Liam gave a grim nod.

"I'll join ye in the courtyard in a few minutes." Broden linked his fingers with Kendra's. "I'd like a few minutes alone with my betrothed."

Liam and Graeme hauled the still struggling Narcissa from the chamber.

The minute the door closed, he pulled Kendra flush to his chest and claimed her mouth in a blistering kiss. She wrapped her arms around his back, holding him every bit as tightly as he held her.

Several breathless moments later, he lifted his head. "Dinna ever do anythin' so foolhardy again, my love. My heart nearly stopped when that bitch pointed the gun at ye. I couldna think of life without ye, and I feared ye'd be taken from me before I ever made ye mine. Or I told ye how verra much I love ye. Love yer soft gray eyes and stubborn chin. Yer glorious hair and luscious curves. Yer obstinance and kindness and generosity and yer untamable spirit."

She cupped his stubbly jaw with her hand, her eyes wide

and luminous, her lips rosy from his fervent kisses. "Do ye truly love me?"

"That's all ye heard of my fine speech?" He chuckled and gave a wry shake of his head.

A smile crept across her mouth. "Och, the rest was lovely, as were yer kisses, but ye've never told me ye loved me."

She stood on her toes, pressing a reverent, sweet kiss to his mouth.

"I do, lass. I have for so verra long, and I couldna tell ye because ye loathed me."

"I didna loathe ye. I realized some time ago that ye stirred things in me I didna understand. Didna ken what they were, and they made me uncomfortable. I think I've loved ye since I was a wee lass toddlin' around after ye."

He cradled her, relishing her warmth and her scent. "Ye *will* marry me."

It wasn't a question.

She tilted her head, an eyebrow cocked. "I shall? A lass rather prefers to be asked than ordered to wed."

He growled and nuzzled her neck. "Will ye? Gift me such an invaluable treasure as ye by my side all the days of my life?"

"I shall if ye will do the same for me."

Releasing her, he frowned. "Can I impose upon ye to stay with my wards? I ken ye havna met them yet, but as my wife, ye'll be a vital part of their lives too. I want them to come live at Glenawayshire. To start over. They'll need time to heal after their mother is—gone."

Kendra bowed her head. "She will hang, willna she?"

"I dinna see any other recourse."

He tilted her chin upward. "Are ye sure about weddin' me? I come with five lasses who barely ken me and will be recoverin' from a tragedy nae bairn should ever have to endure.

Things may no' be easy in the beginnin'. Mayhap no' for some time."

"Broden McGregor, I'll take ye any way I can have ye." She gave him a little push. "Now be off. I'll go to the girls and introduce myself and keep them entertained while ye deal with the other unpleasantness."

A smile worked its way across his face, and he brushed a thumb over her cheek. "Thank ye."

A sharp knock echoed at the door. "We're ready, Broden," Bryston called.

Kendra caught his hand. "Come see me when ye return. No matter how late. I need to ken ye are safe."

THIRTEEN

Kendra brushed a strand of pale blonde hair off Amaryllis's face. Poor dear. The eldest, she knew something was amiss. She'd finally fallen into a fitful slumber about fifteen minutes ago.

The sweet but energetic lasses had bombarded her with questions when she'd entered the nursery almost seven hours ago. She'd mentioned nothing about their mother and had introduced herself as Broden's betrothed.

Their governess and nurse eyed Kendra speculatively but had been polite if a bit reserved. Likely they understood full well that as the wife of the girls' guardian, she would have much input on whether they retained their positions.

She'd excused them both to take a couple of hours for themselves and had earned grateful smiles and, she hoped, allies. She'd need all the help she could muster to take on the task of raising the girls.

"I'm retirin' now," she whispered to Nurse, who was sitting by the fire and knitting.

The woman glanced up, her friendly expression encouraging Kendra. "The young misses took to you, Miss Mackay.

That's not typical. Except for the eldest, they are generally quite shy with strangers."

Hands on her hips, Kendra arched her back. She was unaccustomed to romping about on the floor playing all manner of games and make-believe. "I'm glad."

The nurse put aside her knitting and slowly gained her feet. She was of an age when she really ought to retire, but many in service didn't have the resources to do so. Kendra had no idea what the woman's wages were, but, at the very least, a younger woman should be hired to assist her.

She'd speak to Broden about it.

When he returned.

Of its own accord, her gaze gravitated to the small clock on Amaryllis's nightstand. Nearly nine. It shouldn't have taken this long for Broden and the others to return. Something must've gone wrong.

She'd sent word to the men guarding the countess to double-check and make sure all of the doors to the house were locked.

Nurse approached Kendra. After a covert glance to the sleeping girls, she motioned for her to step into the room she shared with the governess. Miss Postelwaite glanced up from the papers she was grading, her eyes owlish behind her spectacles.

"We wondered if we might have a word with you, Miss MacKay." Nurse exchanged a hesitant glance with the governess.

"Yes, quite," Miss Postelwaite said, setting aside her spectacles before rising. She folded her hands primly before her. "As I'm sure you can guess, we've heard... That is, the other staff report..." She drew in a large breath, her chest expanding. "There's really no tactful way to ask. Is it true the countess is behind the plot to assassinate Lord Montforth?"

Kendra shifted her attention between them. "I think it best if you speak directly to his lordship regarding the matter."

Nurse swallowed audibly and, after Miss Postelwaite gave her an encouraging nod, she ventured closer to Kendra. "We've"—she gestured between herself and the governess—"long suspected she might've had something to do with the previous earl's demise."

And her sons' demises too.

Kendra didn't feel it was her place to apprise them of the repugnant facts. Particularly not with the girls a few feet away and within hearing distances if they should wake. "I'm sorry, but, again, I must defer to Lord Montforth. I'm certain he will explain all as soon as he's able."

With a friendly smile, she made her way to the bedchamber she'd been shown to earlier. As she'd requested, a bath had been prepared and someone had even procured a nightgown for her. She fervently hoped it wasn't one of the countess's.

After bathing and washing her hair, she sat before the fire brushing the strands to expedite their drying. Despite her determination not to, her attention gravitated to the clock. Another hour had passed, and still there'd been no word.

Had Broden returned and decided it was too late to see her?

No, he wouldn't do that. Any more than she'd do the same to him.

Sighing, firmly banishing her vivid imagination to the far corners of her mind, she set aside the hairbrush and closed her eyes. Resting her head against the chair's high back, she relived the past couple of months.

So much had changed.

She was in love. In love with the most magnificent man.

His absence these past weeks had been almost unbearable.

What was it about being in love that made a person's soul yearn for its other half? This time when they'd parted, it had felt like her heart had been carved from her chest. That it wouldn't beat a steady rhythm until she was with him once more.

A soft scratching at the door had her eyelids flying open. *Broden. Och, thank God.*

She jumped from the chair and raced to the panel. Her hand on the latch, she paused. It wouldn't do to open the door wearing nothing but the light nightgown if someone else stood outside. "Who is it?"

"'Tis me, love. Open the door."

With a small cry of delight, she flung the door wide open and launched herself into his arms before he'd completely crossed the threshold. "I was so worried," she said, peppering his jaw and throat with hot kisses. "Did ye catch Oswald?"

He stiffened for an instant. "We found him, but he didna surrender willingly. He took his own life rather than face the hangman's noose."

Honestly, she couldn't blame him.

"I'll tell ye all the details tomorrow, but right now..." He nuzzled the sensitive spot below her ear. "I have more important things on my mind."

He smelled divine: Fresh soap. Shaving lather. His distinct musky maleness. He'd bathed, and his hair was yet damp. He wore only a fine lawn shirt and breeches.

Giving him a coy look from beneath her lashes, she ran her hands over the bulging muscles of his arms. "Why, Lord Montforth, are ye here to seduce yer betrothed?"

"Aye. We'll marry on the morrow, but I mean to introduce ye to pleasure tonight." With a hungry growl, he lifted her in his arms and kicked the door shut behind him.

Kendra was in no frame of mind to summon false protestations of modesty or decorum. She wanted him too. Feverishly.

He laid her upon the turned-down bed, then stood back, hands on his lean hips, his smoldering gaze raking over her. "How could I have been so blind for so long?"

He sat upon the edge of the mattress and reverently ran his forefinger over her cheek, across her mouth, and down her jaw, the column of her throat, and, lastly, to the tidy sky-blue ribbon tied demurely at her bodice.

The smile arcing her mouth held invitation. She wanted their joining every bit as much as he.

"Ye've been a treasure right before my eyes all this time," he murmured, veneration in his voice.

She caught his hand and brought the palm to her lips. She kissed the firm, calloused flesh, breathing him in. "I was just as blind, Broden. But I'm so grateful we see at last." Eyeing him, she propped onto her elbow. "Are ye comin' to bed with yer clothes on?"

His eyes darkened to liquid passion, and his mouth quirked into a seductive smile that held a promise she couldn't wait for him to fulfill.

In a few agile movements, he'd stripped himself bare. Standing beside the bed, he bent one knee and, hands hanging loosely at his side, he patiently waited for Kendra to finish gawking.

"Oh, my."

She dashed a swift glance upward, admiring the wide expanse of muscled chest and rippled abdomen, lingering for a moment on the fresh pinkish scar marring his shoulder. But her attention gravitated back to the rigid evidence of his arousal jutting toward his flat stomach.

She swallowed. Not from fear but unadulterated lust.

Scrambling to Kendra knees, she swiftly untied the ribbon

securing her gown's light fabric and then, raising her gaze to his, pulled the garment off over her head. The coolness of the room swept over her, but no embarrassment or shame assailed her.

Proudly, she remained kneeling, affording him the same opportunity to study her form as he'd permitted her. Then he was laying her onto her back, his eyes, hands, mouth, and body worshipping her.

And she wanted to crawl inside him, to appease the pulsing ache growing and growing and *growing* inside her. She returned every caress, eagerly exploring the sinewy planes and contours of his spectacular body.

His tongue slipped into her mouth, and she greedily sucked as he slowly—maddeningly—teased her with taunting plunges. As he settled between her thighs, she drew her legs up, wrapping them around his waist.

She tore her mouth from his, moaning, "Please, Broden. Please."

He nipped her shoulders before grasping her buttocks with his big hands and tilting her hips. "I love ye, lass. Ye are mine. Now and forever, Kendra."

"Aye," she groaned as the head of his penis entered her. Filling and stretching. God, it felt so good. "Aye, now and forever."

Then, awash with bliss, he took her to the heavens. When the sun exploded behind her eyes and her body convulsed with untold pleasure, she cried over and over, "I love ye, Broden. I love ye."

Much later, or perhaps it had only been a few minutes, he withdrew from her and drew the bedcoverings over them. She snuggled into his side, one arm resting across his ribs and her thigh atop his.

"That," she breathed, still groggy with passion, "was beyond amazin'."

"Aye. 'Twas." He kissed her temple. "Ye are amazin'."

"Can we do it again?" She cracked an eyelid open. "I found it most enlightenin'."

A rough chuckle exploded from him. "I see I've found myself a lusty wife." He ran his tongue over her shoulder, and she gasped, arching into him. "No' that I'm complainin', mind ye. Give me a few minutes to recover, and I'd be delighted to *enlighten* ye again."

She grew serious and propped her chin on his chest. "Broden, Mother says marriage isna easy, even when ye love yer spouse. Promise me, we'll never let anythin' come between us. That we will share our thoughts and feelin's, and never go back to shuttin' each other out. Never be adversaries like we were, bent on hurtin' each other."

He turned his head, scrutinizing her beloved face. "I promise, *leannan*. We're startin' with a ready-made family, and the lasses will require patience and understandin'." He squeezed her buttocks before lacing his fingers with hers. "But together, with our love as an unshakable foundation, we can build a life for them and ourselves."

Giving her a wicked wink, he pulled her atop him. "Now, let's enlighten ye a trifle more."

EPILOGUE

Glenawayshire, Scottish Highlands
June 1728

Kendra relaxed upon the blanket spread beneath the chestnut tree, ten-month-old Keenan asleep beside her with his little fist tucked beneath his chubby chin. The remnants of the family picnic had been haphazardly stuffed inside the hamper, and now her children romped with their father.

Amaryllis, a beautiful young lass on the cusp of womanhood, held Allina's wee, plump hand. At almost four, she quite adored her five adopted older sisters. The girls doted on her and seven-year-old Boyd, who, at present, was proudly showing his papa an insect of some sort.

She adjusted her position, her belly seven months swollen with another bairn, making her feel very much like a whale. A beached whale.

That first year had been a time of transformation for her and Broden. Their marriage had been delayed a month due to the countess's suicide within hours of being confined to a servant's chamber. Claiming she felt unwell, she'd requested tea and asked not to be disturbed until morning.

Liam had found her.

She'd broken a teacup and slit her wrists without ever seeing her daughters again.

She and Oswald had chosen to take their own lives rather than face a trial and certain hanging.

Broden and Kendra had hidden the truth from the girls.

To this day, they didn't know the countess had killed herself, nor that she'd murdered their father and brothers. Perhaps someday, when the girls were adults, if they ever asked questions, the truth might be revealed.

Though what good it would serve, Kendra failed to see.

The former countess hadn't been a particularly doting mother, and it wasn't uncommon for her to go days without ever seeing her daughters. They'd been told she'd become terribly ill after consuming bad fish and had passed from food poisoning.

Naturally, they'd grieved as children do. Even when a parent was negligent, and in the former countess's case, stark raving mad, their children loved them. It had taken several weeks before the lasses warmed up to Broden, but he'd eventually won them over.

Three years ago, after asking Amaryllis, Bergenia, Celosia, Dianella, and Eustoma if they'd like to be adopted by Broden, and receiving enthusiastic affirmations, they'd officially become Broden and Kendra's daughters.

The lasses were already daughters in their hearts. The documentation just made it legally so.

Grimacing, she smoothed her hands over her distended belly.

Soon, she'd be a mother to her ninth child: five adopted and four from her womb. She loved them all the same.

Giving her head a slight shake, she smiled. All those years ago, when she'd been hardly older than Allina, and she'd shadowed Broden's every move, she never could've conceived the happiness the two of them would now share.

Yet as a wee lass, she'd craved his company. Perhaps even then her soul had yearned for its mate.

Broden waved, and after accepting a fistful of wildflowers from Allina, strode toward the blanket. He folded to his side and presented Kendra with the childish bouquet. "Allina picked flowers for ye."

Kendra accepted the mashed blooms as her attention moved over the girls and Boyd wandering the meadow. "I wish yer mother had lived to see her grandchildren."

Broden laid his head in her lap, taking care not to disturb their sleeping son. "Aye. She'd been ill for a long while and kept it hidden from me."

She'd died within six months of their marriage.

Running her fingers through his light brown hair, she perused his beloved face. The babe chose that moment to kick vigorously, and Broden chuckled. "I'll wager yer carryin' another wee son. He's very active."

"He is, indeed," she said, trying to bend to kiss him. "Ugh. I'm so huge that I canna even kiss my husband."

Being a wise man who'd seen her through three previous pregnancies, he sat up and spread his palms over her tummy. "No' so verra huge. I adore seein' yer belly rounded with my child growin' within ye." He waggled his eyebrows. "I also quite like the puttin' the bairn there business."

Kendra laughed. She quite liked that part too.

Cupping her nape, he pressed his mouth to hers. He tasted of berry tarts and wine. As always, even far gone in her pregnancy, her bones liquified at his practiced touch. Sighing, she slipped her arms around his neck, giving in to the moment.

Girlish giggling and a wee lad's offended voice declaring "That's disgustin'" ended the all too short romantic interlude.

Opening her eyes, Kendra observed her brood crowded around the blanket, staring at their parents. A blush tinted the four older girls' cheeks. Allina and Eustoma looked curious, and a repulsed grimace crinkled Boyd's face.

Broden laughed as he released Kendra and shifted to tousle their son's hair. "Ye willna think so when ye are older."

"Lasses are gross," Boyd declared. Then, seeing the offended looks his sisters leveled him, amended his opinion. "Sisters arena, but other lasses are."

"Mama, tell us again how ye and Papa met," Allina said, crawling into her father's lap.

The other children settled onto the blankets, expectancy in their eyes.

"Again?" Kendra sent Broden a helpless glance. "Ye've heard it so many times before."

He took her hand and kissed the knuckles. "Aye, but nae one ever tires of hearin' about true love and happily ever afters."

If you'd like to leave a review, please scan the QR code.

Keep reading for a free preview of
TO DEFY A HIGHLAND DUKE
Heart of a Scot Series, Book Six

TO DEFY A HIGHLAND DUKE

Scottish Highlands
29 December 1720

I'm out of my mind for agreeing to this. Completely and utterly mad.

With that peevish thought, her fingers ice-cold despite her gloves, Marjorie Kennedy shivered and burrowed further beneath the weight of the heavy coach blankets. Only the crown of her soundly sleeping daughter's head peeked from within the cocoon she'd swaddled six-year-old Cora in.

On the opposite seat, her sister-in-law, Berget Kennedy, also buried in a swath of thick coverings, cuddled Elana, Marjorie's seven-year-old daughter.

The bricks now skidding around the coach floor had long since lost any semblance of heat and had been abandoned as foot warmers. Wishing for a roaring fire to warm the soles of her feet, Marjorie wiggled her cold toes against the bottom of her sturdy shoes.

"I canna imagine 'tis much farther, Marjorie." Every bit as exhausted and miserably cold as she, Berget offered a weak upward sweep of her mouth, empathy shining in her kindly gaze. "The last time we stopped, Graeme vowed we'd arrive within the hour."

With chipped teeth, bruised bums, and our blood frozen solid.

Well, Berget might not be frozen through and through. Her bright eyes and flushed cheeks, and the smoldering glance her husband bathed her with when they'd emerged from the inn's private parlor, suggested Graeme had found a creative and effective way to warm his young bride.

Overseeing her daughters' use of the necessary behind the posting house meant Marjorie had never completely thawed before the troupe reboarded the coach and lurched away on the rutted excuse for a road.

It wasn't precisely envy that pricked her, for she didn't begrudge Graeme and Berget their happiness or love. True, Graeme resembled her dead husband Sion strongly and, for a brief period, she'd developed a *tendre* for him.

But the sentiment hadn't been love. He'd reminded her so much of Sion, and she did so miss her husband.

So, *what* precisely, was this disgruntlement chafing her? Abrasive and persistent.

If she must put a name to the aching, fluttering behind her breastbone, she'd call it yearning. For what she'd once had and mightn't—*probably wouldn't*—ever have again: the love and devotion of a strong, loyal, devoted husband and father.

Could one grieve such things?

Love. Devotion. Companionship.

Should one?

How could she not?

Her heart and spirit had wills of their own these days.

Burying her fingers deeper in the furs, Marjorie attempted to ignore her discomfort while keeping her complaints constrained to mutinous musings. Vocalizing her displeasure served no useful purpose, since naught could be done but endure the remainder of the bone-rattling trip.

Besides, it wasn't her nature to be churly or snipe.

This journey, however, reinforced her abhorrence of coach travel, which was why her last prolonged trip had been from England as a bride of eighteen. Starry-eyed and bubbling with hope and expectations as the young bride of Laird Sion Kennedy.

She'd been blessed with three and a half joyful years with Sion before he'd died, far too young, five years ago. Her brawny, strapping husband felled by a gash. A stupid infection of his foot that had turned putrid and poisoned his blood, claimed the doctor.

Sion had left her a widow at two and twenty, in a new homeland, with an infant, a toddler, and a shattered heart and broken spirit. Her daughters were what kept her going.

Maternal pride blossomed in her chest as she swept a love-filled gaze over the sleeping lasses. Thank God for Elana and Cora. She didn't know how she would've borne the grief and loneliness without them.

The constant rumbling, jerking, and bouncing of the coach had whittled her mischievous daughters' good humor to grumpy pouts and, eventually, frustrated tears before slumber claimed the pair. Experience had taught Marjorie that they would awaken energized and quite ready to engage in more shenanigans.

For certain, the propensity for impishness came from their Scots blood.

"I'm quite looking forward to a hot bath and a steaming cup of tea," Marjorie admitted, realizing she'd forgotten to respond to Berget. Tiny, frosty puffs accented her words and emphasized precisely how frigid the temperature had become inside the coach since the sun began its slow descent behind the Highlands' craggy horizon.

A tot of bracing brandy or whisky in the tea wouldn't go amiss either.

"Aye, I do too," came Berget's muffled reply.

Hours of trundling along in this inhospitable weather had chilled Marjorie to the marrow. A glance out the coach's window revealed a cranky, charcoal-gray sky. She pulled her mouth downward and leaned forward a couple of inches, then clamped her teeth together in another bid to tamp down the wave of frustration billowing upward from her chest.

Perfectly wonderful.

If she weren't mistaken, and she'd lived in the Highlands long enough to know she wasn't, those pregnant clouds portended snow.

Had Berget noticed too?

Mayhap that accounted for the single crease between her russet brows, the only indication she was less than satisfied. Berget hadn't uttered a word of protest during the lengthy journey, and she'd been traveling longer than Marjorie. Her sister-in-law was a saint and had become a good friend in recent months.

She and Graeme had returned from Liam and Emeline MacKay's Yuletide house party to collect Marjorie and her daughters for the trip to Trentwick Castle.

Marjorie sincerely believed she would've been half-mad by now had she been required to jostle about in a conveyance as much as Berget had the past few months.

And yet her sister-in-law remained as cheerful and patient as ever. Marjorie couldn't help but admire her daughters' former governess's stamina and good nature. It was no wonder Graeme had fallen in love with Berget.

Fending off the beginning of a headache, Marjorie pressed

two fingers to the bridge of her nose and wondered for the umpteenth time why she'd agreed to spend Hogmanay at Trentwick Castle.

Not just Hogmanay, but a full week of festivities, God help her. A week amongst strangers. More on point, in the home of the Duke of Roxdale.

Loneliness and boredom, that's why.

Pshaw. She silently but emphatically disregarded the impudent thought. *Utter twaddle.*

She was the mother of two adorable, vivacious daughters, and she lived with her charming brothers-in-law, Graeme and Camden Kennedy, kind-hearted Berget, and a good-sized, devoted staff.

She most assuredly was neither lonely nor bored.

The pair of red-haired minxes currently—*blessedly*—sleeping soundly made certain of the latter. As for the former? Well, Marjorie refused to contemplate it. Widows with high-spirited daughters had other things to occupy their time and thoughts.

Neither, however, was she contented.

Eyeing the pewter, slightly pink-tinged sky, she schooled the frown once more trying to pull her mouth downward at the corners. Most definitely snow. Marjorie almost rolled her eyes heavenward in silent rebellion.

Had that devil, the Duke of Roxdale, summoned the foul weather? *Nae.* Devils preferred roaring fire, not snow.

Despite her determination otherwise, a sigh filtered past her lips.

All they needed was to be snowed in with the austere, ill-disposed Keane Buchannan, Duke of Roxdale.

To think, last summer—*for all of five foolish minutes*—she'd believed him disarming and interesting. *Before* his true colors had emerged. Rather, his true personality. Surly. Dour.

Judgmental. His midnight severe brows pulled together and thunderous censure heavy in his arrestingly beautiful hazel eyes.

The devil cannot have beautiful eyes, she argued to herself. *No? Well, that one does.*

Probably to enchant his victims into sinning like the sly serpent in the Garden of Eden.

With deliberate intent, and perhaps the merest thrust of what she considered a too-square chin, Marjorie pointed her thoughts in another direction and stared out the grimy window.

In the freezing mist, she could make out the outline of Graeme's huge horse plodding along to the right of the team.

Always mist and fog and rain and gray. Yet, she'd grown to love the Highlands.

Her brothers-in-law preferred to ride, rather than stuff their large frames into a cramped coach. Not that she blamed them. Towering well over six feet and boasting legs and arms to rival small trees, each was as out of place in a conveyance's small confines as an elephant in a canary cage. But surely, they must be half-frozen themselves, even if they were Scots and accustomed to the cold clime.

A particularly powerful shiver scuttled up Marjorie's spine, spreading across her shoulders and raising the flesh. Shuddering, she silently cursed the weather, her sense of duty, and, most of all, the domineering man she'd encounter all too soon.

Come now, she chided herself, *are you going to allow the likes of that bounder to keep you in a temper?*

Aye. The duke abraded her worse than scraping her naked bottom upon splintered wood.

Hunching lower in the blankets' folds, Berget offered a sympathetic smile.

Marjorie's frustration must've shown in her expression despite her efforts to appear unperturbed.

Trentwick Castle cannot be much farther. It cannot. Marjorie hoped as she clamped her teeth against another shiver and burrowed into the furs pulled to her ears.

This gathering would be the first time the feuding Kennedys and Buchannans had marked Hogmanay together in over three decades. Roxdale's father had impregnated Graeme's aunt, and Gordan Buchannan had been forced to marry Winifred Kennedy at blade point. She'd been as reluctant a participant as the old duke.

According to Camden, family lore claimed his aunt had wept copiously throughout the ceremony and, all the while, the fifth duke had vehemently vowed he'd never bedded the lass. She'd died a mere month after giving birth to Roxdale—some said from a broken heart.

Roxdale's strong resemblance to his sire—the entire ducal lineage, in truth—refuted the old duke's adamant claims that he hadn't fathered the bairn.

Henceforth, the families had avoided each other. Until now.

And she was to blame, in part.

Blast her interference and attempts at peacemaking.

I hope you enjoyed this free preview of
TO DEFY A HIGHLAND DUKE
Heart of a Scot
Book Six

I never know what interesting tidbits I'll come across while researching and writing my historical romances. One of the things that frequently is asked of me is why I choose to use the specific Scots-speak that I do in my HEART OF A SCOT series.

I attempt to insert just enough to give the story the flare I want without bogging down the tale. I think of it like seasoning when I cook. A little enhances the flavor, but too much is unpalatable. I also defer to my editor's suggestions since producing the best book possible for my readers is of utmost importance.

I took a liberal license in introducing hot milk punch. Nothing in my research indicates the beverage was actually served during the period of my story. I do know, however, that hot toddies and other medicinal uses of spirits were commonplace. My characters quite enjoyed the hot milk punch.

Another fact I'd like to address is the recovery period for gunshot wounds. Many things factor into recuperation, including the location of the wound, depth of penetration, the health of the victim, and the skill of the physician treating the patient. Since Broden was a strapping fellow, I permitted him a swift recovery. After all, my story needed to move along.

Unfortunately, in eighteenth century, women were little more than chattels with very few rights. In the case of Narcissa, as unjust as we view it today, she wouldn't have been appointed her daughter's guardian. Unless she had money of her own—highly unlikely, since a woman's property became her husband's upon their marriage—she'd have been totally dependent upon the new heir.

Typically, the crown claimed the entailed assets of a title if no further heirs were forthcoming. Unentailed property could be bequeathed to non-male heirs.

I enjoyed writing TO ENCHANT A HIGHLAND EARL, and I hope you found a few hours of relaxation reading Broden and Kendra's story. If so, be sure to check out the other books in my HEART OF A SCOT series.

To make sure you don't miss any of my book news, subscribe to my newsletter (Get a free book too!). I also have a fabulous VIP Reader Group on Facebook, Collette's Chéris. If you're a fan of my books and historical romance, I'd love to have you join me. You'll also be the first to see new covers, read exclusive excerpts, be the first to know about contests and give-aways, help me pick titles and name characters, and much, much more.

Please consider telling other readers why you enjoyed this book by reviewing it as well. I also truly adore hearing from my readers. You can contact me on my www.collettecameron-books.com and while you are there, explore my author world.

Hugs,
Collette

If you haven't joined Collette's exclusive mailing list click on QR image to sign up! You'll get access to exclusive content, sneak peeks, contests, giveaways, and more...
(P.S. No spam!)

https://collettecameronbooks.com/freegift

Collette loves to hear from readers.
You can contact her via her website: collettecameron-books.com.
Or email her directly at collette@collettecameron-books.com.

You can also follow Collette on social media:
Facebook: https://www.-facebook.com/ColletteCameronNovels/
Instagram: https://instagram.com/collettecameronauthor/
Goodreads: https://www.goodreads.com/collettecameron
Book Bub: https://www.bookbub.com/authors/collette-cameron

Pinterest: http://www.pinterest.com/colletteauthor/
YouTube: https://www.youtube.com/@ColletteCamero-nAuthor

Giggles are Guaranteed
Collette's Cheris Reader Group

https://www.facebook.com/groups/CollettesCheris/

If you love to chat about all things romance-book related and enjoy taking part in fun and engaging live events, contests, and giveaways join **Collette's Chèris VIP Reader Group, https://www.facebook.com/groups/CollettesCheris/,** my exclusive private book group on Facebook.

Giggles are guaranteed!

I Iopc to see you there,
Collette Cameron®

ABOUT THE AUTHOR

COLLETTE CAMERON®

USA Today Bestselling author Collette Cameron® is renowned for her captivating, humorous, and heartwarming Scottish and Regency historical romance novels. With over 65 published titles, over 1.6 million books sold around the world, and multiple writing awards to her credit, Collette is a well-known author in the world of historical romance.

Readers love her witty and relatable characters including daring rogues, dashing scoundrels, and the strong and spirited heroines who capture their hearts. From the rugged highlands to the refined drawing rooms of Regency England, Collette's novels will transport you to another time and place, where love and adventure are just a page away.

Collette's Sweet-to-Spicy Timeless Romances® are the perfect escape for readers looking for romantic escape, poignant inspiration, engaging humor, and entertaining stories.

Based in the Pacific Northwest, Collette is surrounded by the lush greenery and rainy skies that inspire her writing. She dreams of one day splitting her time between the Pacific Northwest and Scotland. In the meantime, she indulges in her love of all things cobalt blue, dachshunds, chocolate, and of course, crafting her next historical romance.

Blue Rose Romance® LLC
collette@collettecameronbooks.com
collettecameronbooks.com

A December with a Duke — Book 3

What Would a Duke Do? — Book 4

Wooed by a Wicked Duke — Book 5

Duchess of His Heart — Book 6

Never Dance with a Duke — Book 7

Wedding Her Christmas Duke — Book 8

The Debutante and the Duke — Book 9

Loved by a Dangerous Duke — Book 10

How to Win a Duke's Heart — Book 11

When a Duke Desires a Lass — Book 12

My Dearest Duke — Book 13

~

FOR THE LOVE OF AN EARL (Wicked Earls' Club)

A Humorous Aristocrat and Wallflower

Regency Romance Adventure

Earl of Wainthorpe — Book 1

Earl of Scarborough — Book 2

Earl of Keyworth — Book 3

Earl of Renshaw — Book 4

~

HEART OF A SCOT

A Passionate Enemies to Lovers

Scottish Highlander Historical Mystery

Romance Adventure

To Love a Highland Laird — Book 1

To Redeem a Highland Rogue — Book 2

To Seduce a Highland Scoundrel — Book 3

To Woo a Highland Warrior — Book 4

To Enchant a Highland Earl — Book 5

To Defy a Highland Duke — Book 6

To Marry a Highland Marauder — Book 7

To Bargain with a Highland Buccaneer — Book 8

A Christmas Kiss for the Highlander — Book 9

HIGHLAND HEATHER ROMANCING A SCOT: CASTLE BRIDES

A Passionate Enemies to Lovers Second Chance

Scottish Highlander Mystery Romance

Heart of a Highlander — Prequel

The Viscount's Vow — Book 1

The Highlander's Heiress — Book 2

The Earl's Enticement — Book 3

Triumph and Treasure — Book 4

Virtue and Valor — Book 5

Heartbreak and Honor — Book

Scandal's Splendor — Book 7

Passion and Plunder — Book 8

Wishes and Wonder — Book 9

A Yuletide Highlander — Book 10

~

LADIES OF OPPORTUNITY
A Bluestockings and Rogues Opposites Attract
Regency Mystery Christmas Romance

The Wallflower's Wild Wager — Book 1

The Spinster's Secret Stake, Book 2

Better Not Bet a Bluestocking – Book 3

~

SECRETS OF SCANDALOUS LADIES
A Romantic Class Difference Forced Proximity
Regency Romance with Aristocrats

A Lady's Scandalous Kiss — Book 1

No Lady for the Lord — Book 2

Love Lessons for a Lady — Book 3

His One and Only Lady — Book 4

Never a Proper Lady — Book 5

Lady Tempts a Rogue — Book 6

~

THE CULPEPPER MISSES
A Humorous Wallflower Family Saga
Regency Romantic Comedy

The Earl and the Spinster — Book 1

The Marquis and the Vixen — Book 2

THE HONORABLE ROGUES®
A Second Chance Redeemable Rogue
and Wallflower Regency Romance

www.ingramcontent.com/pod-product-compliance
Lightning Source LLC
Chambersburg PA
CBHW072133300726
48975CB00003B/1046